The Ivy Crown

Gill Vickery

Five Leaves Publications

www.fiveleaves.co.uk

The Ivy Crown
by Gill Vickery

Published in 2010
by Five Leaves Publications,
PO Box 8786, Nottingham NG1 9AW
www.fiveleaves.co.uk

The Ivy Crown was first
published in 2001
by Hodder Children's Books
© Gill Vickery, 2001, 2010

ISBN: 978 1 905512 85 0

Five Leaves is a member of Inpress
(www.inpressbooks.co.uk)

Cover design © Darius Hinks

Typesetting by
Four Sheets Design and Print

Printed in Great Britain

*For Elizabeth
and Tom*

Acknowledgements

Thank you to Peter Farnell and Adriana White for translating Paganini's letter, and to David Snelling for showing me round his workshop and sharing his knowledge and enthusiasm. Thank you also to Ruth Symes and Patricia Elliott for encouraging me to submit the manuscript. And, finally, thank you to my sister, Shirley, for sending the stamps.

The House in The Hollow

As the taxi reached the top of the hill the huge orange moon floated in front of the windscreen, poised like a third head between Megan's little brother and the taxi driver.

'There's The House,' the driver said.

Megan stopped watching the red figures on the meter and looked out of the window. She smiled, in spite of herself, suddenly understanding why Dad had been so secretive about The House. He'd wanted it to be a surprise. And it was. The House lay cupped in a deep hollow scooped out of the forest. Battlements frilled its domed central tower and its two stubby wings. A turret reared up from one side as if it were trying to escape the sea of clustering trees. Warm yellow light filled rows and rows of long, slot-shaped windows.

'Dad didn't say it was a castle,' Megan said.

'It's not a castle,' Brand said.

'Yes it is.'

'No it's not. It's too small.'

'Whatever.' Megan let him have his own way. In her head she said stubbornly, It is a castle. A very little, ridiculous castle.

The taxi steadily descended the hill between the woods. Megan was glad she was safe from the trees looming outside.

'It's got a moat,' Brand said.

Like a castle, Megan thought. 'Yes,' she said.

'How come you're staying at The House?' the driver asked.

Megan wasn't going to tell him that, not everything anyway.

'Our dad's an artist and he wanted to get away somewhere peaceful to work for a bit.'

That was true, as far as it went. And Brand wanted to come to this house too. He'd said so when Dad asked him. If Dad had ever thought to ask her she'd have told him she hated the idea of leaving the city to come and live in the back-end of nowhere for three months. That's why she'd phoned all her friends from the train, to stay in touch as long as possible. She should have watched the credit on the mobile though: using it up meant she couldn't phone Dad to find out why he hadn't been there at the station like he'd planned. And to make matters worse she'd let Brand exhaust the battery playing games on the train. He hadn't been able to concentrate on reading and it seemed only fair to take turns with him. Now she wished they hadn't used it at all.

Oh Dad, Megan fretted. Where are you?

The taxi stopped at the bottom of the hill, at the end of the road between the woods.

'This is as far as I go,' said the taxi driver.

That surprised Megan; she'd thought the taxi was going to stop by the little bridge over the moat.

Brand scrambled out while Megan handed over the fare. 'I'm sorry there's no tip. I haven't got any more money.' She hadn't expected to pay for a taxi.

'That's OK. D'you want me to wait to see if your Dad's in?'

'No thanks. He said if he wasn't back, he'd make sure Alyson, the housekeeper, stayed.'

'All right. Take care now.'

The taxi driver didn't sound too sure. His eyes flickered briefly, nervously, towards The House just before he turned the taxi and drove back up the hill. Megan frowned. Surely he couldn't be scared of The House? It was too silly: a house playing a role in an old-fashioned horror movie, or posing as a subject for one of Dad's drawings.

6

The taxi dwindled to a humming sound on the other side of the hill, then even that was gone.

In the moonwashed darkness ancient trees surged to the edge of the road like a whispering crowd waiting to advance.

A withered leaf swirled down and rattled on the road.

Megan snatched up her bag and turned to follow Brand as he dashed across the bridge over the moat, climbed the stone steps to the door and hauled on a huge iron bell-pull.

Deep inside, the heart of The House jangled.

Brand yanked again.

Jangle — jangle — jangle.

'Why isn't anybody coming? What are we going to do?'

Megan waved a large, black key. 'Dad sent us this, remember? Just in case of emergencies.'

'Is this an emergency?' Brand's eyes glittered in his pinched little face.

'Not really,' Megan soothed. 'The housekeeper probably hasn't heard us.' She wished she believed herself.

She slotted the key into an oversized escutcheon. The key was heavy and ornate, like a stage prop. She wasn't convinced it would really work.

It turned silently and the door swung open with scarcely a whisper.

Brand rushed inside. 'Hi! We're here!'

The only response was a faint echo: Here! Here!

Megan followed, shutting the door behind her. She dropped the bag, pulled her coat tight against the chill and looked around the panelled hall.

'Isn't anybody here?' Brand asked.

Megan had no idea. 'We'll go and look. Where shall we start?'

She watched Brand take in the details of his surroundings: the spacious, square hall; its central flight of stairs fenced with curly iron bannisters; a landing at the top dividing right and left; a narrow gallery painted with dancing figures under a glass dome.

The glowing moon loomed through the dome like a giant's eye peering downwards.

'That way.' Brand set off to the right towards a door set in a shadowy alcove. A shape hung from the door at about head height.

Megan followed, her trainers squealing faintly on the tiled floor.

Brand stopped abruptly and Megan collided with him.

'What's the matter?' she said.

He ignored her and stretched up his hand to the thing hanging from the door.

It was a violin, its bow slipped behind a posy of dried flowers twined round its elegant neck.

Pity and anger and resentment jostled inside Megan. It wasn't fair! Dad should have told her. He should have taken the violin down before Brand saw it.

But Brand was smiling. His hand reached up to the satiny, golden-brown instrument. His fingers touched lightly, drew away.

His smile widened to a grin. 'Touch it, Megan!'

Puzzled, Megan ran a tentative finger down the violin. 'It's not real!'

The graceful contours were a flat, painted plane under her hand. Every shadow, every string, every flower, painted in exquisite, perfect detail.

'I wonder what it sounds like,' Brand said.

'It doesn't sound like anything, it's only a picture.' Megan spoke more sharply than she meant to.

Brand's grin vanished. 'I mean the real one. The one this is a picture of.'

Megan grasped the doorknob. It was embossed with a laughing face. She twisted it. The face went upside down and its expression changed from laughter to despair in a single turn. Like Brand, she thought and opened the door. 'Come on.'

She led the way down a dim corridor panelled in black wood and carpeted in scarlet. At the end of the corridor was another door, slightly open, with a wedge of light prising its way out of one side. It was warm, amber light that coaxed a tang of woodsmoke and spices along with it.

On the other side of the door a huge kitchen stretched the whole width of the house. Everything in it, cupboards, dresser, stove, sink, fireplace, was oversized. Shadows from lamp and firelight made them sway as if they were alive.

Brand nodded towards a scrubbed wooden table standing four-square in the middle of the room: 'Is that for us?'

'Two places. It must be,' Megan said looking at the things laid out on a checked cloth covering one end of the table: white bread, butter, cheese, cherry cake and orange juice. A baby's supper, she thought with scorn.

At least food would distract Brand for a while.

They washed their hands at the stone sink. It was so high even Megan had to raise her arms to clear the edge and water trickled down to her elbows. Brand balanced on his toes turning the soap slowly in his hands, building up a froth of tiny bubbles. 'Where's Dad? Why wasn't he at the station?'

Megan dried her hands and began making herself a cheese sandwich. She answered carefully: 'Maybe ... the car broke down.'

'Why didn't we see it on the way then?'

'He probably went a short cut, on a side road.'

'But why isn't he back?'

Megan wished Brand hadn't asked. She was worried about that too. And what about the missing housekeeper, Alyson? Where was she?

Megan balanced a slab of cherry cake on her knife and held it out to Brand. 'This looks good.'

A jaunty tune jingled loudly from somewhere. Megan

jumped. The cake hit the floor scattering yellow crumbs and a scarlet cherry.

Darkness lurched and firelight set the copper pans winking.

The tune warbled insistently on.

Megan and Brand looked wildly round the room. Megan saw the mobile phone first, sprinted to the dresser, snatched up the phone.

'Hello?'

'Megan? It's Dad.'

An Unexpected Message

Relief bubbled through Megan. Everything would be all right now. 'Dad! Where are you?'

'Stuck out on the road. The car's in a ditch.' Dad's voice faded, came back: '...you two OK?'

Brand tugged at Megan's arm. 'Let me speak.'

She hastily suppressed the impulse to push her little brother away and keep Dad's reassuring voice for herself. She leaned towards Brand instead and tilted the mobile so they could both hear Dad.

'We're fine,' she said before Brand could say anything. 'Are you?'

'Yes. Can I speak to —.'

'When are you coming back?' Brand interrupted. His voice wobbled with the effort of trying not to cry.

'Soon, I hope,' Dad said cheerfully. 'Don't get upset, Brand. I'll be quick as I can.'

'I'm not upset,' Brand fibbed. Megan gave him a hug and a smile for being so brave. She stood up straight.

'How long do you think you'll be?' she asked.

'I don't really know.' Dad spoke softly so Megan knew he didn't want Brand to hear. 'I might be all night at this rate. The road's isolated and I couldn't ring for help because I'd left my mobile behind.'

'Never mind,' Megan said, trying to make it seem unimportant that Dad's memory hadn't been so good over the last few months. 'At least it was here for us to use. What phone are you using?'

'Someone stopped to help a few minutes back – he's lent me his. I tried your mobile but I couldn't get anything.'

'Sorry. The battery's dead.'

'I need to speak to Alyson. Can you get her for me?'

'She isn't here. The House was empty when we arrived.'

'But she was supposed to wait until we all got back! Has she left a message?'

'I don't think so.'

There was an angry-sounding indrawn breath — then silence.

'Dad?'

'Look, the guy I borrowed the phone from can't wait. I've got to go. Lock up carefully and...'

Megan knew what was coming next.

'...look after Brand.'

She always did. 'I will. Bye, Dad.'

Brand tugged at Megan's arm again. 'I want to talk to Dad!'

Megan handed him the phone. 'Be quick, he's got to go.'

She let Brand chat while she scooped up the crumbled piece of cake. By the time she'd cut another slice Brand had switched off the phone. He bounced back to the table. 'I'm hungry.'

Whatever Dad had said to Brand had cheered him up.

'Here.' Megan pushed the piece of buttered cake over to him. Brand was happy at the moment, that was all that mattered for now.

Megan shivered. The room was getting chilly. She crossed to the fire, unhooked the poker from a set of fire-dogs and prodded the almost burnt-out logs. The grey husks crumbled, releasing a shower of golden sparks from their dying hearts.

Megan looked at the poker more carefully. 'This is a cat.'

'Looks like a poker to me.'

'And the tongs are a bird and the brush's a bat. Even the stand's a tree.' She held up the cat. 'The top's a head, the long bit's legs, and the bottom part's paws.'

The cat snarled up at brother and sister, its ears flattened, its eyes black slits, Megan turned the face away.

The paws she'd thrust into the fire were tipped with curling claws, like iron scimitars, smeared with ash.

She put it back on the stand and picked up the bird-shaped tongs. She squeezed the elongated beak and it opened and closed with a peculiar clanking like a ring full of jailer's keys knocking together as he walked.

'I think this is meant to be a raven,' Megan said doubtfully, 'sort of like a crow only fiercer.'

She hung it back on its branch. It swung there for a moment, creaking.

Brand leaned forward: 'There's a face in that tree.'

'Where?'

'In the middle. Under the lumpy bit halfway up the trunk.'

A sad, rather lovely, face peered up at Megan from beneath a twisted knot.

Brand yawned.

'Bed,' Megan insisted, 'but we ought to lock up first.'

She helped Brand haul a firescreen in front of the hearth. It was heavy, with metal foliage. Megan could see little faces everywhere among the leaves. She didn't stop to see what they were the faces of, not this late at night.

She and Brand picked up the pots from the table and dumped them in the sink until morning. Megan felt really tired now, her eyes gritty and sore.

One last job.

As she bent over the sink to pull at the wooden shutters her reflection leaned towards her from out of the night-darkened glass. Megan paused to regard her grave, unsmiling expression. Misery, she thought. But then, there hadn't been a lot to laugh about over the last year.

She tried an experimental smile.

An old man peered over her shoulder.

She let go of the shutters and spun round.

'What's the matter? I'm only helping.' Brand teetered on a chair he'd dragged up to the window and caught at the swinging shutters.

'You startled me, that's all.' Megan pressed the shutters flat and clicked the latch into place.

There must be some fault in the glass, Megan decided, and it warped Brand's reflection, made him look old and angry. She watched him stretch forward, his thin arms unfolding. He's so like Mum, she thought, nothing like Dad — big and bulky, and comforting, usually. Megan wished Dad was with them. She was tired of looking after Brand on her own. Tomorrow, Dad would be back tomorrow. She could manage till then.

She let Brand lead the way out. He stopped at the end of the corridor in front of the painted door and stood on tiptoe with his nose almost touching the violin.

'What are you doing?' Megan asked.

'There's a label painted inside. You can see it through that sound hole.'

Megan wasn't sure what to do. Brand might get upset if she said the wrong thing. The trouble was she didn't always know what the right thing was, even if Dad thought she did.

Cautiously she tried, 'What does it say?'

Brand squinted. '...anno 1732, I.H.S. and a sort of cross shape sprouting leaves.' He skewed his head down over one shoulder. 'I can't see properly. It's too shadowy.' He was beginning to sound anxious.

'Leave it for now then,' Megan said gently. 'Try again tomorrow, in the daylight.'

Out in the hall the moon had rolled its orange eye around and was spying from the other side of the glass dome.

Megan put her hand on the newel post of the iron bannister. She found she was gripping a bronze owl. It had one eye open like the moon.

At the top of the stairs the west wing was brightly lit, the east wing a gaping blackness like a mouth waiting to be fed. They turned left, to the west.

'Look!' Brand dashed up to a door and pulled off a yellow stick-up note with a little drawing of himself saying, 'My room! Keep out!!!' He flung the door open and ran inside.

Megan went to the next door along. She snatched the note from it and crumpled it up. Dad had drawn her as an angel.

She was Megan, just Megan. Nothing more: nothing special. If only Dad would see her that way instead of some kind of heroine.

Brand stuck his head out of the door. 'Where's the bathroom?'

'Let's go and look.'

When they found it at the end of the corridor it took Megan by surprise. It was completely modern, basic and small. Unlike her bedroom. Tall lancet windows — thankfully already shuttered — rose loftily on either side of an empty fireplace large enough to stand up in. A mountainous wardrobe swaggered against one wall and a stretch limo of a dressing-table parked against another. It was all out of scale, like the kitchen.

Megan climbed up on to a four-poster bed swathed in gold brocade curtains on three sides. She bounced experimentally.

A door appeared in the forest of roses sprawling over the walls and Brand burst through.

'Connecting doors,' he announced and jumped on to the bed, lifting Megan a little like a boat bobbing on the sea. 'How d'you think Dad found this house?'

'In some newspaper advert I suppose. It's quiet, isolated, hasn't got a phone ... exactly what he wanted.' She slid off the bed making Brand drop into a trough.

'Time for you to go to sleep.'

He allowed her to guide him back to his room and kiss him goodnight. His eyes began to drift shut straight away.

Megan crept through the connecting door and closed it

15

softly. Brambles grew unbroken over the wallpaper forest once again.

She pulled her things out of her bag and changed quickly, strewing clothes over a fat brocade chair at the foot of the bed. Its lion's feet looked ready to run off with her belongings.

She decided to leave the light on.

She released the curtain on the fourth side of the bed and it fell into place, enclosing her in a fabric box. Enough light filtered through to illuminate her room within a room. Burrowing deep under the covers, Megan remembered how, when she was very young and Brand not much more than a toddler, they had often made a den out of the dining-room table and a pair of old curtains. In its haven they had shared adventures, secrets and baby sorrows. Now, in this place, she was alone with a sorrow too deep for comforting.

In Megan's dreams the curtain opened. A sigh moved the air around her face. It felt like a cool hand stroking her forehead. A tall shape leaned over her. 'Go away, Dad,' she whispered. The figure drew back and let the curtain fall.

Into the Woods

Megan woke to the sound of mourning. Wind sighed in the chimney and shutters rattled like bones.

She opened her eyes. The wind cried again. Half-asleep, Megan breathed, 'What's wrong?'

The crying went on.

Suddenly wide awake, Megan sat up and remembered everything. 'Dad!'

She scrambled out of bed, wincing as the cold wooden floor shocked her bare feet. She island-hopped from rug to rug until she reached a sea nymph washstand simpering in the corner. 'A lick and a promise,' she told it as water gushed into the shell basin balanced on the sea nymph's head from taps pretending to be dolphins.

Washed and dressed, Megan half-skipped to the wall and banged cheerfully on the wallpaper forest. 'Come on, Brand. Breakfast.'

He didn't answer.

She searched for a handle to the invisible door. There wasn't one, not even one disguised as something else.

She went into the corridor. Brand's door stood wide open and she could see his room was empty. He must have gone down to the kitchen on his own, driven by hunger and given confidence by knowing Dad was back.

'You could've waited for me,' Megan grumbled at her absent brother and set off after him.

The shadows in the east wing had turned from black to grey. Shivering, Megan hurried into the sunshine falling through the glass dome on to the landing and over the stairs. At the bottom she swung from the owl perched on its newel post. Golden light winked in its bronze eye.

'You should be asleep,' Megan lectured it. 'You're meant to be nocturnal.'

It winked again.

Megan's stomach rumbled fiercely and she ran the rest of the way to the kitchen. It was empty and suspiciously tidy. All the pots and cutlery had been washed up and put away somewhere. A single place setting was laid out on the table with a piece of paper tucked under the plate. In Brand's loopy scrawl it said: *Gone to the woods with Alyson.*

Alyson. The housekeeper.

First she wasn't at The House when she should have been, then she appeared and took Brand away with her.

Megan read the note again. Nothing about Dad. So he hadn't got back last night. She must have dreamed him in her room.

She ate breakfast, then picked up the pen Brand had dropped next to his note, and added: *Dad, I've gone to find Brand. Love Megan.*

The golden woodlands were nothing like the clotted darkness of last night. They were open and well-lit, letting the sun shine warmly on Megan's face as she walked into them.

She kicked at a pebble sending it rolling down the path. She ran after it feeling all at once like a little child again, free, able to do as she pleased. The rattle of the pebble and the pad of her feet mingled with the sounds of birdsong, soft rustlings and, faintly, the noise of running water. Intrigued, she set off towards the watery sounds. They led her to a narrow river with a well-worn track running along its bank.

Megan's confidence grew: keeping to the track meant she could always find her way back. If she hadn't been so anxious about Brand she'd almost have enjoyed herself. She couldn't though, not when Brand was missing with this strange Alyson.

She walked on calling, 'Brand! Brand!'

There was no answer.

Megan imagined what Dad's reaction might be when he read the note in the kitchen. He wouldn't be angry that she'd lost track of Brand, he'd be sad and apologise for asking her to shoulder a burden that wasn't really hers to take up. And the guilt and anxiety in his eyes would wound her terribly.

Megan didn't notice the path narrowing until it disappeared altogether. Surprised, she stepped on to the grassy track taking its place and looked round. The river turned abruptly left, slanting noisily away over steep rocks glistening with wet moss and trailing weed like drowning hair.

She couldn't decide which way to go: by the river — which would be easy to follow without getting lost — or along the grassy pathway winding between the trees. Being streetwise was no good here.

She decided on the path between the trees, it was lighter than the way by the water.

After a while the path began to twist and turn, looping round clumps of trees. Undergrowth and bracken sprang up clogging the open spaces. The path petered out altogether. The forest had become a wild wood. None of the trees here were like the well-mannered limes and planes of her city home; apart from holly and oak she couldn't recognise any of them. The most common sort had the brightest leaves, burning gold against dark branches draped in ash-grey moss. A short distance away, on the edge of a swathe of bracken, was a vast old tree covered in strange drooping red flowers.

Surely trees didn't flower in the autumn?

Forgetting Brand she ploughed through the bracken towards the tree. It stood apart on a grassy hump, red toadstools clumping round the base of its gnarled old

19

trunk and fleshy warped ears of yellow fungi sprouting from its bark.

The flowers were strips of rag. Dozens and dozens festooned its branches.

Megan circled the tree. The rags were tied all round it. Mystified, she squinted up trying to see how far the strips went. They seemed to go almost to the top.

'Hey!' a voice shouted.

She turned.

Coming towards her was a man. He was too far away for her to make out his expression but the way he moved showed he meant to catch her.

Her heart lurched. All the warnings she'd ever heard about strangers flooded into her head: she was alone, in an isolated place, and a man she didn't know was after her!

'Wait!' he shouted and leaped in high foolish bounds over the knee-high bracken.

Megan ducked behind the old tree and ran into the woods. She ran and ran, zigzagging blindly between the trees. She raced down a hollow filled with leaves, waded frantically through them, scrabbled up a slope on the other side. At the top she tripped, jumped up, launched herself away again, flying through the trees. She splashed through a patch of bog; mud sucked off a trainer. She stopped to try and pull it free, risked a look behind her.

Something moved in the undergrowth — a bird shot upwards screaming in protest She left the shoe and ran again further into the woods, deeper and deeper.

A bank loomed in front of her, steep, covered in brambles. She couldn't run up it; she had no breath left.

Abruptly her legs folded. She fell back against a tree and slid down it, the bark snagging at her coat, letting her down in a series of jolts.

Sounds of her own panic filled her ears: heart drumming, blood pulsing, breath rasping.

She screwed her eyes shut and hugged her arms round herself to ease the stitch in her side. Gradually it lessened and the noises of her body quietened.

From the shelter of the tree she risked another look round. There was no sign of the man. Cautiously she stood up, slowly, quietly, and listened. She could hear only the rhythmical sighing of leaves in the canopy above her and a liquid babbling from somewhere over the rise.

The river! If she walked back along its bank she could find her way to The House again.

She climbed awkwardly up the bank hampered by her shoeless foot and the grasping brambles. More rips scarred her coat. She didn't care; she had to get back to The House.

Almost at the top she stopped to catch her breath again. The river noises were clearer from up here; they almost sounded like voices. Very like voices. Voices and moving water mixed up together.

People. There had to be people over there. They'd help her surely? But what if the man was there?

She had to take a chance. She could hide at the top of the rise and spy down on whoever was talking.

She climbed the last couple of metres, crossed quickly over a narrow, rough path of beaten earth winding along the top of the rise and looked down from behind the shelter of a tree.

In front of her a gentle slope fell down to the river flowing through a shallow clearing. Ducks bobbed and swirled on its surface. By the bank stood a stone cottage, sun gilding its grey slate roof. A sparkling white fence marched round a neat garden at its front and hens scratched absent-mindedly in a wired-off area in one corner.

Standing by the red front door was a woman, talking to Brand.

A glow of delighted relief surged through Megan. She

was safe. She opened her mouth to call out.

A hand tapped her shoulder. 'Hello, Megan.'

She spun round, stared up wide-eyed at the man who'd been chasing her. A smile stretched across his red face and he sounded out of breath as he said, 'I didn't expect to run a race with you.' He lifted up a foot and shook a clod of mud from the bottom one of his shoes. 'I'm not dressed for orienteering.'

She could see that. He was wearing a suit.

'Who are you?' she demanded, hoping the glare she aimed at the man disguised how scared she felt. 'How d'you know my name?'

He pulled a silky handkerchief out of his pocket and dabbed at his forehead. 'I'm Brian Walmsley,' he said.

His name meant nothing to Megan.

'I brought your father back this morning,' the man went on. 'He asked me to come and look for you while he waited at The House. I'm the Midlands manager of The Sanctuary Trust — they own the house you're staying in.' He smiled. 'When I saw the direction you were running in I realised you'd end up here and I turned off down an easier way.' Fastidiously he flicked a small yellow leaf from the sleeve of his jacket. 'It was a longer way round but it avoided the brambles.'

Megan stepped back, away from Brian Walmsley and down towards the little cottage. She yelped as a sharp thing pierced her foot.

The man held out her missing trainer pinched between his thumb and forefinger. 'You lost your shoe.'

Megan slid it on and began to hobble down the rise as fast as she could. Brian Walmsley offered his arm for support. Megan ignored it and carried on down the bank. Hurrying to keep up, Brian Walmsley slipped and landed flat on his back in the undergrowth. Half-choked with giggles, Megan yelled, 'Brand!'

'Megan!' Her little brother sprinted towards her. The

22

woman started to follow him. Behind her Megan heard the man struggle to his feet among the snapping undergrowth.

The woman stopped abruptly, drew back a step.

Brand hurled himself at Megan as if he hadn't seen her for days. 'What are you doing here?'

'Oh, just going for a little ramble. What do you think, idiot? I was looking for you.'

She limped down to the flat, arm round Brand's shoulders, with Brian Walmsley stumbling after them. Hope you tear your posh suit, Megan thought.

They walked towards the cottage to where the woman waited.

'I don't know why you came after me,' Brand said. 'I was with Alyson. I left you a note.'

'That didn't tell me much,' Megan grumbled.

'I'm Alyson,' the woman said. Her voice sounded amused, as though she wasn't at all sorry for the worry she'd caused.

Megan turned to face her knowing that she was going to be really rude.

The angry words melted away.

Alyson was the most beautiful woman Megan had ever seen. Not pretty or attractive beautiful, but really beautiful in a way that stood outside time and had nothing to do with fashion or trends: tawny golden eyes glowed, lustrous black hair glinted like preened feathers, the sculpted mouth smiled in a welcome specially reserved for Megan. She felt all this beauty wrap itself round her like a spell of safekeeping. She needn't have worried about Brand. He was quite safe with Alyson.

The housekeeper turned the warm smile on to Brand and held out a straw-lined wicker basket with six eggs nestling inside. 'D'you want to carry these?'

'Yes,' he said, as though whatever Alyson suggested was not only reasonable but also unquestionably right.

Brian Walmsley butted in, breaking the cosy spell. 'I need to talk to you, Alyson,' he said.

Megan looked at him in astonishment. The way he spoke showed he knew the housekeeper and didn't like her very much.

'If you want to.' Alyson immediately started down a broad path reaching out from behind her cottage. Brian Walmsley had to run a few steps to catch up with her. It made him look ridiculous.

'I want to walk with Alyson,' Brand scowled. Megan did too. She wanted to find out more about the housekeeper.

'Tell me about her,' she said.

Brand's face lit up. 'She asked me if I liked The House and I told her I liked the violin on the door and she said, "Why?" and I said because I did music. She was really interested and we talked a lot.'

His face glowed with enthusiasm. It had been a long time since Brand had talked about his music or been happy like this. She let him talk on, enjoying the flow of his chatter. After a while she stopped listening properly and found herself watching Alyson and Brian Walmsley. He kept a space between himself and the housekeeper. He really didn't like her. Well, Megan didn't like him. He'd given her a bad fright chasing her through the woods. And he had no right to talk to Alyson like he did.

They all turned a wide curve. The trees came to an abrupt stop like the hem of a skirt and there was The House in its clearing. Over it a large black bird glided smoothly, coming to rest on the turret.

'Race you to the door!' Megan challenged Brand.

She let him run ahead, over the gravel, across the bridge and up the steps to the door. He touched it first. 'I won!' he panted, his face lit with a huge grin of pleasure.

Dad was going to be so pleased.

24

Out of the Woods

Brian Walmsley was first in the kitchen where Dad waited. 'I found them, Michael,' he announced triumphantly.

They're using first names, Megan thought. For a moment she felt like a stranger at a party, then she was enveloped with Brand in Dad's vast bear hug. She pushed away from the comforting embrace, afraid she might cry.

'I've been worried to death,' Dad said. 'It's a good job Brian found you.'

Brian Walmsley's grin expanded like an elastic band pulled to its limit. 'We'd have been back sooner but when I called out she took off like a scared rabbit. I don't know what she thought I was going to do.'

'She was sensible,' Dad said. 'In her place I'd have done the same thing.'

He sat at the table. Brand squeezed as close to him as he could. Megan sat on the other side, away from Brian Walmsley.

'Why did you take so long, Dad?' Brand said. 'I thought you'd never get here.'

'Like I said on the phone,' Dad began, 'the car ended up in a ditch. It wasn't very pleasant.' He rubbed his neck ruefully. 'I guess I was lucky to escape with whiplash. I swerved to avoid this cat, a great black thing that sauntered out of the dark across the road for all the world as if it owned it. It even came and inspected me when I got out of the car, just like it was curious to know if I was in one piece or not, then it disappeared again.

'I thought I'd have to have wait till morning for help but I was lucky, someone did come by and I was able to phone

25

you and the breakdown service. But then I had to wait the rest of the night for them to find me. I spent it worrying about you two here on your own without Alyson.'

The four of them looked round. The housekeeper wasn't there. No one had noticed her leave the kitchen.

'I've already had a word with her about that,' Brian Walmsley told Dad. 'I expect better of my staff.'

Megan glared, but she supposed Brian Walmsley did have the right to order Alyson around if he was her boss.

'This house is in a funny place,' Brand said, 'right in the middle of a wood.'

'It's in the forest because it began life as a mediaeval hunting lodge,' Brian Walmsley said, 'then it was converted to a manor house during the sixteenth century. It took its present form a hundred and eighty years ago during the Gothic revival.'

Even though he spoke mechanically, as if he were reciting from a book, Megan found herself leaning forward, wanting to know more.

'Alterations,' Brian Walmsley went on, 'were made by the then owner, Henry Devonport. After his wife died in childbirth he came to live here with the infant, Lettice...'

'Lettuce!' Brand laughed.

'Let-*teece*,' Brian Walmsley corrected firmly.

Brand bounced up and down. 'Lettuce! Lettuce!'

Megan saw Brian Walmsley's lips go thin with irritation at Brand's silliness. She didn't like it much either but it was good to see him laughing. Dad ought to stop it though, before Brand went completely over the top. She sighed. She knew he wouldn't. She'd have to divert attention to something else.

'What's the Gothic revival?' she asked.

'It's when people went mad for what they imagined was authentic mediaeval design,' Dad said. 'They plastered every inch of their houses, inside and out, with mock Gothic twiddly bits.'

That explained the strange creatures lurking through-out The House.

Dad went on, 'Henry and young Lettice were particularly fond of things Gothic. They didn't have much taste but Lettice had a lot of enthusiasm and Henry had a lot of money.'

'Indulging the girl's obsessions nearly bankrupted Henry,' Brian Walmsley said.

Megan decided she liked Lettice, and not only because Brian Walmsley didn't approve of her: she sounded lively and strong-minded, someone who wasn't afraid to say what she wanted and stubbornly insist that she get it. Megan had been like that once, but not now.

'Henry had the dome done and the tower stuck on,' Dad said, 'and crenellated the walls so they looked like battlements. Then, he converted the west wing into a ballroom and invited all his friends up from London to show them how clever he'd been.'

'A ballroom! I've never seen a ballroom! Show me, Dad,' said Megan.

'Later,' he said. 'I've got to go into Stretton now and see if my hire car's ready.'

'I want to come,' Brand said.

'Me too,' added Megan. The ballroom could wait for a bit. If she went into Stretton she might be able to find out more about Lettice and this weird old house without letting slimy, disapproving Brian Walmsley know she was interested.

'OK,' Dad said, 'and we'd better get you a new coat, Megan. That one's about had it after your adventure in the woods.'

'I need to go and change my shoes first.'

Dad followed her out of the door. Megan wondered what he was going to say that he didn't want Brand or Brian Walmsley to hear.

'Thanks for going after Brand.'

'What else could I do?'

'You could've waited here and left him to it.'

'I might as well have, he was perfectly all right.'

'This time, yes.' Dad's eyes were troubled.

Megan turned from them.

As she reached the end of the corridor Dad called, 'Don't be long.' His voice sounded miles away and nothing to do with her.

Upstairs Megan threw her filthy trainers to one side and rummaged around in the giant wardrobe until she found another pair. It had been a good idea for Dad to come a week early and get most of their stuff in while they stayed behind with Gran.

Megan peeled off her dirty socks and folded them together. She needed the bath to dangle her grubby feet in.

In the corridor, from the open door of the bedroom opposite, came the sound of someone singing. The melody was simple and as sweet as a daisy.

Curious, Megan paused in the doorway of her bedroom. A sensation like cold breath on the back of her neck made her look back over her shoulder.

There was nothing there. She shivered. Old houses were always full of draughts. She scrubbed at her skin, rubbing the cold feeling away as she crossed the corridor. The room facing her was obviously her father's: his clothes were strewn all over it. Alyson, her back to Megan, smoothed down bedcovers as she sang. Megan wished she could make out the words.

She tapped on the door. 'Excuse me.'

Alyson turned and presented Megan with her wonderful smile though her eyes focused elsewhere, at a spot somewhere behind Megan.

Before Megan could give in to the impulse to turn round and see what she was looking at, the housekeeper gathered up a bundle of bed-linen heaped on a chair and said, 'I'm off to the utility room with this lot. Have you got any washing?'

'Only my socks. They got mucky in the woods. Like my feet.'

'Your right one looks a bit sore,' Alyson said. 'A good soaking might do it good.'

Megan wriggled her toes. 'I'm just going to do that.'

The housekeeper took the socks from Megan. 'I'll put these with the rest of the wash. If your foot's no better tomorrow let me know. I've got some herbal remedies you can use.'

Megan relaxed in the warmth of Alyson's concern. 'I will.'

The housekeeper went downstairs with her bundle of washing and Megan went to the bathroom. She sat on the side of the bath paddling her feet in the water. It soothed away her anxieties along with the dirt. Dad was here now so she didn't have sole responsibility for Brand. Perhaps staying at The House wouldn't be that bad after all.

Megan hummed as she cleaned out the bath and hummed back in her room while she changed into clean socks and trainers. By the time she got downstairs the tune had slipped from her mind. Megan could never hold a melody in her head for long. It was a shame, Alyson's tune had been so pretty.

A furious honking sounded from outside telling Megan that Brian Walmsley was getting impatient. She deliberately walked slowly. Let him wait!

It wasn't that far to Stretton, but the journey took longer than she remembered from last night. The autumn trees went on for miles. She leaned forward and tapped Dad on the shoulder. 'How big is this wood?'

'Not sure. Huge. Brian, you're the expert, what do you say?'

'I don't know the acreage though I think we're on a par with Sherwood. I believe they were once part of the same vast Midlands forest in the olden days.'

Olden days! Megan stifled a giggle at the old-fashioned, fairytale phrase.

Brian Walmsley didn't notice. 'Almost there,' he said.

The trees thinned. Houses appeared. A sign flashed by:

STRETTON MAGNA WELCOMES CAREFUL DRIVERS.

Megan wondered if that included Dad.

The Witch of Stretton Magna

There wasn't a lot to look at in Stretton. In spite of the 'Magna' after its name it was only a little town with the usual shops, a couple of churches, and a library and tiny local museum jostling for space in one building.

The car stopped in a cobbled square set in a small apologetic market. 'You kids get out here and I'll take Mike to the garage,' Brian Walmsley said.

Dad hated his name shortened. Megan expected him to jump down Brian Walmsley's throat but he only said, 'I'll meet you two back here in an hour.'

'I want to go with you,' Brand said immediately.

'D'you mind?' Dad asked Megan.

'No,' she lied and got out of the car.

Dad took some money out of his wallet and passed it to Megan. 'Go and buy that new coat.'

'Thanks.' Megan stepped back and Brian Walmsley drove off with her father and brother. She waved a brief goodbye.

No one waved back.

Even though it stung that Dad spent more time thinking of Brand than of her it had one advantage: Brand thought he'd hurt Mum, hurt her really badly, and while Dad spent so much time trying to convince him that he hadn't, he was too preoccupied ever to discover the terrible thing Megan had done.

She should be grateful for that at least.

Fashion choice was limited in the little town. Megan tried all three clothes shops before choosing the least horrible coat on offer. She was glad no one from school could see the sensible jacket she ended up with.

She glanced at the church clock. Half an hour gone already! She hadn't meant to spend that long choosing a coat, not when she wanted to find out about Lettice and The House. She couldn't discover much in the thirty minutes she'd got left and the choice of where to find information was even more limited than where to find clothes.

I'll try the library first, she decided.

It wasn't very inspiring, just a large room with a few bays of books. At first Megan thought it was empty then she noticed a girl sitting on the floor, tucked away behind one of the bookcases.

She checked her watch. Only twenty-four minutes to go. She'd better get to the museum quickly.

Its door had a faded handwritten poster pinned to it ... *Roman, Saxon and Mediaeval finds ... The Witch of Stretton Magna ... The World Wars ... The Mothers' Union embroidered hassocks ...*

Inside an elderly attendant slept at a desk near the door. Megan walked quickly past him and an assortment of exhibits on the World Wars with gas masks leering from the walls and limp khaki uniforms swinging from stands like the victims of a hangman. The bits of Roman pottery and cracked mediaeval tiles didn't really interest her. She turned a corner into a room housing the embroidered hassocks. Unexpectedly enchanted by the glowing colours, Megan lingered. She imagined lines of the kneelers with their doves and lambs, flames and stars cheering up the cold grey stone of a church floor.

Almost reluctantly she left them and turned into a narrow annexe leading to the next room. Two pictures hung there, one on either side, facing each other. Small brass plaques gave details.

Megan came eye to eye with *Sir Walter Devonport, JP. 1602-1689.*

Devonport — that was Lettice and Henry's name!

32

This man must be an ancestor. Megan wondered if either of his descendants resembled him. Looking at the heavy, cold face, framed by its long curling wig, she hoped not.

Megan turned to see who Sir Walter was staring at so contemptuously. The picture on the opposite wall was completely different from his suavely painted portrait: it was a crude black and white woodcut of an old woman in a baggy dress and tiny, pointed boots. The nameplate read, *Judith Moone, Witch of Stretton Magna. Accused by Jacob Fisher, sentenced by Sir Walter Devonport. Burned 31 October 1645.*

Thickly cut lines showed the warty crone surrounded by animals drawn all out of scale. By the witch's knee sat a labrador-sized cat with spiky black letters over its head spelling out the name, *Pywackett*. Next to it stalked a bird, big as an eagle, with the name *Hodge* under its talons. In a corner clustered a clump of bats labelled, *The Knotted Cloude*.

Megan examined Judith's face under its shapeless cap more closely. If she ignored the clumsy way it was drawn she could see that the witch wasn't all that old, not ancient anyway.

A long scroll curling from her mouth like one of Dad's cartoon speech bubbles proclaimed, *I am Judith Moone, a witch.*

Megan tried to feel sorry for the poor woman. She couldn't.

Grief choked her heart; there was no room in it for anything else. Besides, there was no point — the witch and those who might have mourned her had vanished centuries before. Megan wondered how long grief went on possessing you. Hers had clawed at her for half a year. It felt as if it would be with her for ever.

Most of the last room in the museum was filled with a display of documents, except for a red velvet curtain that covered the back wall. A notice invited visitors to press a large brass button.

Megan pressed. The lights dimmed.

The curtain slowly glided back revealing the tableau of a crowded courtroom, ill-lit and musty. A woman, her dress a splash of scarlet, shrank back in the dock while a man, face full of hatred, pointed accusingly at her.

From nowhere came the sound of voices and cries: accusations, pleas, the bang of a gavel, the subdued murmur of excited voices.

The noises faded and a slow, disembodied voice said, 'What you see in front of you is a scene from the trial of Judith Moone, damnable witch of Stretton Magna in the county of...'

The voice began to slow down. 'In the autumn of 1645 ...' The voice slowed still more and deepened: '... Jacob Fisher ...' The voice became a distorted growl: '... Sir Walter Devonport and ...' With a guttural mumble the voice slurred to a halt.

'Oh, great!' Megan said. Half a story was really, really frustrating and she didn't have any time left to talk to the attendant. She'd have to come back to find out the rest of Judith's tale.

And she'd found out nothing at all about Lettice.

She wondered if she ought to tell the attendant that the tableau display had broken down. When she saw he was still asleep she crept out without waking him. She smiled a bit to herself as she slipped by: he hadn't seen her go in or come out so he might think magic was responsible for drawing back the red curtain.

Dad and Brand were waiting by the granite war memorial in the square.

'We're going to a tea shop,' Brand told her. 'It's called Polly's Pantry.'

'Sounds a bit naff.'

'This is a minor market town, not a throbbing metropolis,'

Dad said. 'There isn't anywhere else that serves afternoon teas. Besides, it does very good coffee and decent cakes. And I'm hungry.'

They set off across the square towards a narrow dark side street marked, Hob's Lane. A thin autumn wind swept coldly by, scurrying a swirl of leaves like little brown mice down the winding lane of crooked old houses. Trapped in a miniature vortex they spun in the doorway of an elegant building standing straight among the squat, bent houses.

'It's the same,' Brand said pointing to a painted sign hanging from a pole jutting out above the shiny black door of the house.

He was right; over neat gold lettering reading, 'Magna Strings', was a copy of the painting in The House: the same violin, the same bow tucked behind at the same angle, the same posy of flowers twined round its neck.

Wind plucked at Megan's ankles. 'Come on, it's cold.'

Brand ran to the shop window. Behind the glass a new violin, glowing russet in a wash of sunlight, lay in a nest of sheet music.

'It's the same,' Brand said again, 'the same.'

The violin in the window was completely different from the one in The House, even Megan could see that. 'No it's not. It's a different colour and a different shape.'

Brand pressed his palms against the window. Slowly his head drooped forward until it rested on the window pane. His breath patched the glass. 'It's the same music.'

Megan couldn't help glancing at the sheets in the window though she knew it was pointless; she couldn't read music.

She looked at Dad, puzzled. 'I don't understand.'

He shook his head to say, leave it, put his hands gently on Brand's shoulders and pulled him away from the window. 'Come on, son. Polly's is just across the lane. Let's go and get those cakes.' He steered Brand towards the tea room door.

A creaking noise, like a bough bending, made Megan glance back. The sign swung in the bitter wind, moaning in protest like an arthritic joint. Light glinted off the gold lettering and gilded the edges of the panelled door.

It opened.

Brian Walmsley came out, turned right and disappeared into the shadows at the far end of Hob's Lane.

The smell of the proper roast dinner Alyson cooked that evening made Megan feel ravenous. She'd only had tea at Polly's Pantry unlike Dad and Brand who'd eaten cakes to cheer themselves up. Brand was all right now. He threw himself into a seat at the enormous table saying, 'Food!' as if he hadn't eaten for days.

'Are you going to eat with us?' Megan asked Alyson.

'No. I eat at home, with my cat.'

'You can have dinner with us,' Brand said. 'Can't she, Dad?'

'Alyson goes home in the evenings,' Dad explained.

'But it's dark!' Megan turned to Alyson. 'Will you be safe, walking through the woods on your own?'

'Perfectly safe.'

'Do you have to go?' Brand asked.

'Not just yet. I want to finish the ironing first.' Alyson headed for the utility room. 'I might stay long enough to see you off to bed, maybe even read a story,' she teased. 'You need an early night being up so late yesterday.'

'Yes!' Brand said.

Dad abruptly pushed a serving dish towards him. 'Here, potatoes — help yourself.'

Megan dug carrots out of a bowl writhing with embossed tendrils of ivy. 'I like Alyson,' she said, 'don't you?'

Dad hesitated: 'Yes, I do, I just don't approve of some of the things she does.'

'What sort of things?' Brand said.

'Like taking you off to the woods without asking me first.'

'She couldn't ask,' Brand said, 'you weren't here.'

'Then she should've waited till I was.'

Brand opened his mouth to protest.

'Eat!' Dad commanded.

Brand did as he was told. He ate so quickly he finished well before Megan and Dad.

'Can I go?' he asked when Alyson came back into the kitchen.

'OK,' Dad said. Brand scrambled down from the table, took Alyson's outstretched hand and towed her towards the door.

A flash of jealousy jolted through Megan. Instantly shame quenched the jealousy. It was horrible to feel like that, like before, when Mum couldn't share herself between them in the way she used to. Then Megan had let Brand take as much attention as Mum had the strength to give, and hated him for stealing her portion.

The housekeeper paused in the doorway. 'Look after your foot,' she said to Megan.

Until that moment Megan had forgotten about it. Now it ached and felt sore. She shifted uncomfortably. 'I'll try.'

Alyson closed the door quietly behind her.

'What's wrong with your foot?' Dad asked.

'It's only a few blisters.'

'I'll take a look at it later.'

'It's all right,' Megan insisted. It wasn't though. Since Alyson had drawn attention to it, it felt really sore.

'I'll have a look anyway,' Dad said firmly.

'Alyson's going to give me a herbal remedy.'

'I'm not sure I'm happy about that. Folk cures can do more harm than good.'

Megan didn't argue. Dad's eyebrows had bunched up in

a frown. He ate mechanically, deep in thought. Silence stretched on. Megan wondered what she could say to break it.

Dancing in the Dark

'Show me round The House, Dad. Show me the ballroom like you promised.'

'You'd see more by daylight,' Dad said. 'Not all the rooms are wired yet.'

'Please.'

'Just downstairs, then.'

They went to Dad's studio first It was in the old dining room next to the kitchen. The only furnishings were his precious drawing table and chair, a long cheval glass and a stool. Paper lay ready on the slanting board and sharpened pencils sat in a trough at the front. All Dad's painting equipment stood neatly stacked against bare, white walls.

'Same rules as at home. No one comes in here uninvited,' Dad shut the door firmly. 'Remember that, and no touching anything in there.'

'I never do,' Megan said, too surprised to be indignant.

'I wish other people didn't.'

Megan couldn't imagine who he meant. There was only her and Brand and neither of them would risk laying a finger on Dad's work. He was very possessive about it. He always reminded Megan of one of those infants who curved their arms around their school work to stop anyone from copying it.

After the studio came a study half panelled in dark wood, half papered in a design of excitable foliage penetrated at intervals by demonic-looking peacocks. Matching curtains hung at the windows. Next to it was a small room with a TV and a corpulent old sofa.

They crossed the corridor again. With a flourish Dad

threw open the door to reveal a library. A proper, old-fashioned library with bookcases covering three walls and an unlit inglenook fireplace taking up most of the fourth. Plaster monkeys in short jackets and tasselled hats cavorted along a frieze around the top of the walls.

Dad put a foot on the fender and gestured upwards to a painting over the fireplace: 'Let me introduce you to the creators of The House as we know it today. I give you Sir Henry and The Honourable Lettice Devonport, lovers of all things Gothic, at their ancestral home.'

The Devonports presented themselves in front of The House as it nestled darkly among the autumn woods. Lettice, clutching a small red book, sat on a rustic bench while Henry stood beside her, his shotgun draped over one arm. Their faces told a different story from their stiffly formal poses. Henry's eyes were shadowed under his wide-brimmed hat and his mouth had a melancholy twist.

'Poor old Henry,' Megan said. She turned her attention to Lettice. There was nothing melancholy about her. Bold, dark eyes stared out at Megan from a pert face, its chin angled provocatively.

'She's the same as me,' Megan said.

'Yes,' Dad said, 'maybe a year or two older but no more.'

That was true but it wasn't what she'd meant. Why didn't Dad see? She knew the answer to that: he didn't see because she wouldn't let him, and anyway, he was too busy with Brand.

All at once the room felt cold. Megan's skin prickled with goose bumps. She wrapped her arms round herself. 'Where next?'

'The ballroom, though there's no lighting in there, so you're not going to see a lot,' Dad warned.

The ballroom was a cavernous darkness. Shuttered windows, outlined with pencil-thin lines of moonlight, ran down three walls from floor to ceiling.

Megan heard Dad stepping confidently across empty

space to the nearest window. A catch clicked and pearly grey light stabbed across the room as he hauled open a shutter. It banged back against the wall sending echoes rolling into the room.

Dad worked methodically until all the shutters down one side were open. Bars of moonlight speared the blackness. Dad waltzed back up the middle of the room, appearing and vanishing as he passed through moonlight to shadow and back again.

He bowed to Megan: 'Will you do me the honour of this dance?'

She curtsied solemnly: 'I will.'

To Dad's hummed waltz they whirled round the ballroom, flickering through light and shade like characters in an old black and white film. They spun round the room, feet pattering over the springing wooden floor, raising a smell of dust and desertion.

Megan felt safe, happy, twirling in the darkness to silent music. It was so long since she'd felt happy. Happy enough to talk to Dad. She lined the words up in her head. Maybe the truth wasn't so bad. Maybe she could risk telling him the thing she'd done — after all, it had been for Brand's sake and Dad would understand that; they both hated to see him sad.

At the far end of the ballroom they stopped dancing.

Megan took a chance. 'Dad, I want to talk to you.'

She felt him hesitate: 'Maybe I ought to check on Brand first.'

A familiar despair swamped Megan's courage taking most of her fragile happiness with it. She made herself try again: 'He's fine with Alyson. He'll probably get a bit mad if she's still reading to him and you go barging in.'

'I suppose so.'

He wasn't really convinced. 'Come on,' Megan said, making herself sound cheerful and confident. She half guided Dad out of the ballroom and across the hall. She stopped in front of the painted door and found herself saying, 'You should've told me about the violin.'

'I was as concerned as you when I first saw it but what could I do? It's a work of art. I couldn't take the door off and hide it in case it upset Brand!'

'You could still have warned me.'

Dad patted her arm. 'You coped. You always do.'

He regarded the violin with what Megan recognised as his artist's eye, concentrating hard, his face impassive.

'What did Brand say when he saw it?'

'He wanted to know what the real violin was like.'

'The real one?'

'He thinks it's a painting of an actual instrument. He tried to read the label inside.'

'That's a good sign, very good.'

Dad was clutching at straws. It meant nothing that Brand was interested in the painted violin.

Dad walked breezily down the scarlet carpet to his studio. He sat in his chair and reached out with his left hand to the trough at the bottom of the drawing board. He frowned. 'Where is it?'

'Where's what?'

'My draughtsman's pencil.'

'It's there, on the right.' That was odd, with Dad being left-handed.

Dad picked it up. 'I wish she'd leave my stuff alone.'

'Who?'

'Alyson.'

'How do you know it's her?'

'It's not you or Brand and there isn't anybody else,' Dad grunted and began drawing.

Alyson probably only moved things to tidy or dust. She wouldn't know how touchy Dad was about his drawing.

Megan pulled up the stool and watched Dad draw a perfect outline of the violin. A few lines more and sheet music fluttered around it like doves. Other lines, other birds:

ravens.

Megan broke her silence: 'Brand said the music in the shop window was "the same". What did he mean?'

Dad pencilled in a vicious eye and a dagger beak. 'It was the piece Mum was trying to get him to learn when she was...'

Dying, Dad. Say it.

'...ill. You know how bad he feels because he wouldn't practise for her.'

What Megan knew was that it wasn't refusing to practise for Mum that Brand felt guilty about, it was how he'd hated being with her those last few weeks. He'd hated and feared the smell in her room; hated the efforts to speak that left her exhausted. And most of all he'd hated the way she looked, melting away before his eyes.

He'd run away and refused to play for her because he was a little boy and afraid. Megan, though, was older and should have known better.

Dad worked a sheen on to the violin. 'All the same, if — as you say — he's interested in the painting on the door I might be able to get him playing again. Introduce the idea and see how he reacts.'

The posy of flowers emerged from a swirl of delicate strokes.

'I wouldn't go that fast if I were you,' Megan suggested cautiously. ' Why don't you wait a bit and see what Brand wants?'

'Wise Megan. Of course we mustn't push him.'

With a flourish the drawing was finished. Dad slid it under a clean sheet of paper and clipped both to the board. 'I must go and check on him now.'

I said I wanted to talk, Megan stormed in her mind, I wanted to talk about me, me, me. Conversations with Dad always turned out like this, always came back to Brand.

She hadn't the heart to protest any more. She might as well go to her room.

Upstairs she wriggled back against her pillows feeling more tired than she expected. She closed her eyes and conjured up the picture of Lettice and Henry. The artist had posed them close to each other, as though he wanted to show they had an affectionate father and daughter bond.

Dreamily Megan wondered what a picture of Dad and her would be like. Their poses would be more casual though Dad wouldn't look that different from Henry, not with all that sadness in his eyes.

What about her? Maybe the artist would see the true Megan, paint her anger and guilt as vividly as the artist of long ago had painted Lettice's boldness. Not if she was careful. In her mental picture she made herself into the false Megan and moved herself and Dad around trying to make a satisfactory composition. No matter how hard she tried Brand always appeared from somewhere and shifted the balance so she had to start again, and again...

The Wishing Tree

'I've got something for you,' Alyson said, turning from the stove where breakfast was cooking.

Megan couldn't imagine what it might be.

Alyson's tawny eyes glittered with amusement. 'It's nothing exciting, just that herbal remedy I promised for your foot.' She passed a brown paper packet to Megan. 'Draw a few inches of water in the bath, sprinkle in half the herbs and soak your foot for about ten minutes. Do the same tonight and I guarantee your foot will be better tomorrow.'

Megan was doubtful. She said, 'Thank you,' anyway, to be polite.

'Do it now while I get breakfast, then it'll be ready when you've finished.'

Megan hesitated. Only Dad and Mum had the right to tell her what to do, knew what was best. But Mum wasn't there to care any more. At least Alyson remembered about the bad foot which was more than Dad had done.

Megan's foot started to throb quite painfully again. She limped off to the bathroom. The infusion did soothe the pain and Megan felt fine by the time she made her way back to the kitchen where Brand was starting on a full plate: fat red tomatoes, mushrooms and bacon.

'How's the foot now?' Alyson asked.

'All right thanks.' She added awkwardly, 'It was kind of you to think of me.'

Alyson's luminous smile drew Megan into its light. 'You deserve a bit of cosseting.' She piled up a second plateful.

Brand leaned back in his chair and stretched out his hand towards the range.

It was only then Megan noticed a huge black cat half-camouflaged by the dark cushion it curled up on.

'Hello, cat,' Brand said.

The cat recoiled, hissing and growling, ears flattened, eyes narrow slashes like slits of yellow silk in black velvet

'Leave her!' Alyson ordered.

'I was only going to stroke her.'

Alyson's harshness died away as quickly as it had flared up. 'She's old and needs keeping an eye on, that's why I let her come into The House with me.'

The cat turned on her cushion a couple of times then settled, tightly wound up, tail twitching fretfully between her front paws.

'Pye's temperamental and it'd be a shame if you got scratched.'

'It's a funny name,' Brand said, 'Pie.'

'It's an old country name, short for Pywackett.'

Pywackett? The same as the witch's cat in the museum picture. Looking at the baleful eyes monitoring Brand Megan decided Alyson's cat was well named.

'I promise I won't bother her,' Brand said solemnly.

'I think that's very sensible.'

Brand beamed at the praise. Megan saw he'd already forgotten that Alyson had snapped at him only a moment ago.

The cat yawned, unsheathed a pawful of claws, gave them a perfunctory lick then slid them back into their tender scabbard. She tucked the innocent paw under her chin and closed her eyes.

After breakfast Megan went upstairs to fetch her old trainers. She bumped into Dad in the corridor. 'Where are you off to so early?' he asked.

'For a walk. We won't be long. And I won't get lost this time.'

'How's your foot?'

'OK. Alyson's remedy worked.'

Dad frowned. 'Come into my room and let me have a look.'

Megan perched on the edge of Dad's bed and allowed her foot to be inspected. He reluctantly satisfied himself that the cuts and blisters were healing perfectly.

Megan slid her sock and trainer back on. 'Can I go now?'

'Yes.' Dad hesitated as if he didn't know how to frame the words he wanted to say next.

Megan knew what was expected of her. 'I'll look after Brand. I don't mind.'

Dad's face relaxed with relief.

Megan gave him a quick kiss. There was surprise in her father's answering smile and though it wasn't full of brilliance like Alyson's, it was warmer.

'Megan! Come on,' Brand yelled up the stairs.

'Coming,' she called back and with a quick wave to Dad, ran down to join Brand.

The sharp, cold day made Megan and Brand walk quickly. Mist swirled round the bases of trees, writhing away to a secret damp silence in the woods. Brand whistled a swinging sort of tune. Megan wished, for the hundredth time, that she shared at least some of her little brother's talent for music.

The sunshine strengthened. Mist began to melt away. Branches dripped steadily, tick-tocking moisture into the fallen leaves. In the clearer light the wood looked familiar.

'This is the way I came yesterday,' Megan said. 'There's a weird tree over there with red strips tied all over it. I'll show you.'

They turned off the path by the river and on to the springy turf.

A noise like the distant sound of a dentist's drill bored its way through the trees.

'What's that?' Brand said.

47

'No idea. Let's go and see.'

When they got to the glade she had crossed the day before they found it filled with the buzzing noise and an acrid smell of petrol. On the far side, near to where the falsely flowering tree flaunted its red blossoms, two men with grass cutters were clearing a wide circle in the bracken. In the middle lay a platform of broad branches stuffed with kindling.

Whirling round, her arms full of twigs, was a girl Megan recognised from the library yesterday. She looks younger than me, Megan thought, but older than Brand.

'What's she doing?' Brand asked.

'Dancing, I think.'

'Funny sort of dance.'

He was right, Megan thought as they watched the girl spinning, her fair hair swirling out in a mass of tiny braids.

Suddenly, in mid-spin, she flung her arms wide and the momentum propelled the twigs over the branches on the ground. The spin stopped, leaving the girl facing Megan and Brand. She paused a moment in surprise then ran over.

'Hi,' she said. 'Are you coming to help with the bonfire?'

'Oh, that's what it is,' Megan said at the same time as Brand said, 'Yes.'

The girl laughed and shook her plaits back over her shoulder making the little golden beads at their ends click. 'My name's Robin,' she said. 'What's yours?'

'Megan.'

'I'm Brand.'

'That's a funny name.'

Brand was used to people saying that. 'It's short for Brandon. Why are you building a bonfire in the middle of the woods?'

'Tradition,' Robin said promptly. 'Loads of people from Stretton used to come and build it and clear the dancing ring; now it's only Dad and my uncle and me. Stretton people still come to the dance on Guy Fawkes night — it's the work before they don't like, they think it's too far to travel. My Dad says that's just an excuse.' A shrewd sort of look crossed her face. 'Do you live near?'

'We're staying at The House in The Hollow,' Megan told her.

Robin gasped; her hands flew up to cover the startled 'o' of her mouth.

'What's the matter?' Brand said.

The grass cutters switched off. In the abrupt silence one of the men called, 'Robin!'

'My dad wants me,' the girl said. 'Are you going to stop and help us?'

'We can't, we've got to get back,' Megan said.

'I want to stay,' Brand said.

Before Megan could start persuading Brand to change his mind Robin said, 'I'll tie a wish on the tree, then you'll have to come back.'

'What d'you mean?' Brand asked.

'You tie a red strip on the wishing tree,' she pointed to the old tree on the edge of the bracken, 'and make your wish, then, whatever you want, you get. See you!' She ran off towards her father, startling a raven bobbing up and down in the clearing. It lifted off with a protesting 'caw' and flapped ponderously away over the trees.

'We'll have to come back now,' Brand said.

'No we won't. I don't believe in rubbish superstitions.' Megan had enough to do without having to bother about strange dancing girls.

'I'm going to ask Dad.' Brand headed determinedly back up the track.

On the way back Megan kept thinking about Robin's reaction when she realised Megan and her family were living at The House. Brand must have been thinking the same thing. When they reached The Hollow he said, 'Why did that girl go all funny when you said we were staying here?'

'No idea,' Megan said. It troubled her though because it reminded her of the taxi driver on the night they arrived and his furtive reluctance to get too near The House.

What did local people know that she didn't?

Dad did give permission for Brand to help with the bonfire, as Megan knew he would, then surprised her by being firm and adding, 'After you've made a start on some schoolwork. We have to keep the authorities happy.'

Dad sat them at a table each in the study and set out books and papers under the scrutiny of the invigilating peacocks.

Brand hunched over his paper and scribbled aimlessly. Megan ignored him and wrote quickly, steadily, for herself — not for school and not, for once, to help blot out the memories: writing down the facts would get them clear in her mind and might just reveal something she'd not noticed before.

She described The House and its transformation from hunting lodge to Gothic manor, then she wrote what she knew about its owners, the Devonports. First there was Sir Walter, the seventeenth-century magistrate whose picture in the museum stared across at the witch he'd condemned to death by burning. Then there were the Victorians, Henry and Lettice. Megan stopped writing and chewed the end of her pen. She didn't know much about them, only what Dad and Brian Walmsley had mentioned yesterday — that Henry was a widower whose wife had died giving birth to Lettice, their only child. Megan wondered which was worse, never to know your mother at all, or to know her, love her, have her love you and then lose her? She couldn't decide.

Brand pushed his paper to one side. 'This is boring. I want to go and do the bonfire with that girl.'

'You know what Dad said,' Megan coaxed. 'Finish a bit of your assignment about this place to keep school happy, then I'll take you back to the woods.'

'I want to go now.'

This was much more like the old Brand: a stubborn eight-year-old having a sulk because he couldn't get his own way. Dad ought to know.

Megan got up. 'I'll talk to Dad.'

She tapped tentatively on the studio door hoping Dad wasn't going to mind his work being interrupted.

'Come in!' Dad bellowed.

The random scattering of rough drawings showed his work was at the messy, incoherent stage when ideas didn't flow smoothly. Megan bet herself he'd be glad of an excuse to stop. She explained about Brand.

'It's working! Coming here *was* a good idea,' Dad said. 'He's getting new things to occupy his mind with.'

So am I, Megan thought, surprised.

Dad put his pencil down. 'You can take him to the woods this afternoon, but first we've got to go to Stretton — I want to fax some work off from that office place by the market square. I'm sure you two can amuse yourselves while I'm busy and then we can all have lunch together.'

Megan's spirits rose: Dad was doing some proper work at last! His agent was going to be pleased. Dad hadn't had any real ideas for months and months. Before, he'd always produced a graphic novel every year.

Megan said happily, 'I'll go and give Brand the good news.'

When she told him he flopped back in his chair, his face sullen. 'If I can't go and help with the bonfire now I'm not going to Stretton.'

'Dad'll be sorry.'

'Good. I'd rather stay with Alyson anyway.'

Megan went back to Dad. He'd have to sort this out.

***

Megan smiled as she made her way out to the car. She was glad, really, really glad, that Brand had insisted on staying behind: even Dad hadn't been able to persuade him to change his mind. He wasn't happy about leaving Brand with Alyson but Megan was. She was going to have Dad all to herself for once.

A Day for Discoveries

Stretton Market was closed. Without it the town was smaller and duller than ever.

'I'm off to fax,' Dad said. 'Where shall we meet up?'

'In the library.' Megan wanted to find out more about The House and its long-ago inhabitants.

She went straight to the young man sitting at the enquiry desk. 'Can I help?' he beamed enthusiastically.

'Please. I'm staying at The House in The Hollow and my school wants me to do an assignment on it. I only know a bit, about Lettice and Henry Devonport making it all Gothic, and I saw in the museum that Walter Devonport had a witch burned in sixteen hundred and something but that's about all. Have you got anything else? About the Devonports and the witch, I mean.'

'Let's go and look.' He took Megan to a bay labelled 'Local History.' It mostly had old hardback books in dull colours mixed up with cardboard holders full of limp pamphlets and out-of-date maps.

'Have you got a website?' Megan asked hopefully.

'Not yet. I'm afraid you'll just have to browse through these.' He waved at the uninspiring books. 'There is this though.' He scrabbled in one of the cardboard holders. 'It's a very good summary of the history of The House by a local author, Brian Walmsley.'

Megan wrinkled her nose in distaste as she took it. She didn't really want to read anything by Brian Walmsley.

The librarian tried again. 'Lettice did write a book you might want to look at.'

'Yes please.' Megan wondered what Lettice could possibly have written a book about.

'I'm afraid it's held in our Central Library. I can request it for you but you'll have to read it here. It's not for loan.'

'Aren't there any other books about the Devonports?'

'Unfortunately they didn't do enough to merit a whole book being written about them! You'll have to dip into some general histories and pick bits out.'

'Is there anything special I can look out for?'

'There's Paganini...'

That was new.

'...He came to stay at The House in the 1800s,' the librarian said, 'to give a concert for Henry and Lettice.'

Megan imagined Lettice dancing in the ballroom like her and Dad last night. But Lettice would have danced in the glowing light of hundreds of candles with happy guests all around.

'What sort of concert was it?' she asked.

'A violin recital.'

The vision of Lettice dancing faded. The picture of the violin on the door took its place.

'Who was he? This Paganini.'

The librarian scribbled on his pad: NICCOLÒ PAGANINI. He tore the page off and gave it to Megan. 'If you need more details you can look him up in the encyclopaedia.'

Megan shouldn't have said the information was for an assignment. The librarian was one of those who made students do their own research even though they knew all about what you wanted.

Megan turned back to Local History: first she wanted to know about the Devonports and the witch, then she'd look up this violinist. Just as she'd chosen two fat books on the history of Stretton Magna to add to Brian Walmsley's pamphlet Dad turned up.

'Glad to see you mean business,' he said, eyeing the fat books. 'Let's go and have lunch and you can tell me what you've discovered.'

Megan liked Polly's Pantry. The trim little cafe felt cosy and safe with its small round tables, its blackened beams and whitewashed walls.

Dad handed her the menu. 'You'll find the lunches a tad more exciting than sausage, egg and chips.'

'That'll make a change. I'm fed up with meat and two veg. I'd do anything for chicken korma or a really good Chinese.'

'Mum loved exotic food. You're just like her.'

Dad was linking Mum with Megan, not himself or Brand. That was a first.

'I know I indulge Brand,' Dad said, 'let him have what he wants, within reason, like comfort food. It's because he's only a little boy. He seems to be over Mum but he isn't, not yet.'

Why can't you see I'm not either, Megan thought behind her mask of sweetness.

'We're older,' Dad said. 'We can cope better.'

Speak for yourself, Megan said bitterly in her head.

'We've struggled through the worst part of our grief. We're managing. Brand isn't, even if he seems to be. You know it's why he won't play the violin any more, because Mum isn't there to listen.'

Megan stared at the pattern of leaves woven into the white tablecloth and said nothing.

' Look, Megan.' Dad leaned forward and took hold of her hands. 'I'm not saying your grief, or mine, is any less awful than Brand's: she was your mum too and my wife. We all loved her.' Dad's eyes glistened. Megan desperately hoped he wasn't going to cry. She turned away.

Dad dropped her hands. 'The difference is that Brand's still a small child. He doesn't understand death in quite the way we do. Don't you remember how he kept thinking in some vague way that Mum would come back? For sports day at school, for summer holidays.'

Megan neatly pleated her paper napkin. 'I thought I saw her in the High Street once. And, when it was her birthday, I went past the chemist's and I thought, I'll buy her some dewberry bath oil, she likes dewberry. It was funny because the moment before I'd been thinking, It's Mum's birthday and I can't give her a present. I'll never be able to give her a present again.'

'You didn't tell me.'

'You didn't ask.'

'Tell me now. Anything, everything.'

Megan panicked. She'd needed Dad's comforting so badly she'd forgotten to be cautious. She couldn't possibly tell him everything. If he found out about her broken promise he'd never forgive her. She'd lose him too.

The waitress distracted them. 'Ready to order?' The friendly woman dressed in a vaguely Victorian costume held a pencil poised above a notepad.

'Lasagne,' Megan ordered quickly.

'Traditional Shepherd's Pie,' Dad added.

Before Dad could pick up the conversation again Megan put her books on the table and unfolded the piece of paper tucked inside.

'The librarian said this man stayed in The House but he wouldn't tell me anything else. Who was Paganini?'

'A famous Italian violinist. The first instrumental megastar. A sort of nineteenth-century Vanessa Mae but nowhere near so pretty.'

'I wonder how Lettice got to meet him?'

'Who knows? She probably heard him play and fell for his charisma like everybody else.'

'I still think it's funny he came to The House. Why would he bother if he was famous?'

Dad shrugged. 'You'll just have to do some more research. Try your library books.'

Megan turned to the indexes. 'No Paganini,' she said in disgust.

She'd have to read Brian Walmsley's pamphlet after all.

In the quiet of her room Megan skimmed through the pamphlet impatiently, determined not to read any more than she had to. She found what she wanted in the index, read intently then hurried to Dad's studio. She was so excited she almost forgot to knock first. Habit made her remember. She rushed in as soon as she heard Dad's grunted, 'Yes?'

'Have a look at this. Brian Walmsley wrote it.'

'In a minute,' Dad spoke without looking up or stopping his drawing.

Megan knew what that meant. 'How are things going?' she asked.

'Pretty good.'

Dad was working on a larger, more polished drawing than the loose scribbles he'd done that morning. 'Tell me what you think of my title page.'

Megan never understood why he wanted to know what anyone thought of early drafts; his drawings changed as he went along and finished illustrations always ended up different from roughs.

The title page did look good though; a melancholy figure stood among swirling mists twining round spiky Gothic lettering spelling out, 'The Revenant'.

'What's that mean?'

'Ghost. A ghost who's trapped between Heaven and Earth.'

'What's your story about?'

'Don't be obstructive. I'll think of one eventually.'

Dad wasn't usually this cheerful at the start of a book. If the story was good the drawings often didn't work well or, if the drawings came first, the story was slow in evolving which often made Dad bad-tempered. Mum said — used to say — it served him right for being the author *and* the illustrator. Megan wondered if Dad remembered how he always snapped back that his own ideas worked out best in the end and anyway, he was paid more for doing both.

'Are you ready for a break?'

'In a bit. I want to finish this.' He turned back to the drawing board. For a while Megan watched the effortless flow of the pencil filling out details of the revenant's clothes, his bony hands, his wild hair. Then Dad set to work on the facial features: straight nose, thin-lipped mouth, sloe-shaped eyes. The long-dead man began to take on a familiarity Megan couldn't place and didn't like.

She glanced at the earlier pictures — people dancing, a crowd surrounding a figure tied to a stake. Even in Dad's artist's shorthand Megan recognised the revenant's face in every drawing. A story was forming in her father's mind though he didn't seem to know exactly what it was yet.

Megan wondered where the story of the revenant had come from and who he was. She didn't ask Dad. If he ever said anything about the mysterious process of creation it was always, 'I've become possessed by the ambience of place.' A critic had written that once in a review of one of Dad's most popular books. He thought it was funny.

Megan left Dad absorbed in his work and went slowly to the study. She wasn't sure she ought to tell Brand what she'd discovered, not without checking with Dad first. She wouldn't have risked it if Brand hadn't been in such a cheerful mood when she and Dad returned from Stretton. He'd enjoyed staying at The House being made a fuss of by Alyson.

Megan sat on the arm of his chair and asked tentatively, 'Do you know anything about a musician called Paganini?'

'A bit. I did one of his pieces for my Grade Three. Mum says he was the first modern virtuoso. Why?'

Dad was right Brand did always talk about Mum as if

58

she were still alive.

'You remember Brian Walmsley telling us about Lettice and Henry Devonport? Well, they met Paganini when he was on tour in 1832 and invited him to give a concert here.' Megan waved the pamphlet at Brand. 'According to Brian Walmsley, Paganini wanted to come here because of the violin on the door.'

'He came to see a painting?'

'Not exactly. It's a picture of the real thing.'

'I told you it was real,' Brand said. 'Alyson said it was too, when you and Dad went off to Stretton.'

'Did she say it was made by somebody called Guarneri Del Gesù?' Megan pronounced the unfamiliar words carefully.

Brand shook his head.

Megan went on, 'Paganini had a Guarneri and he couldn't resist the chance to compare his with the Devonports' violin. Brian Walmsley says they're very rare. They're worth megabucks.'

Brand's eyes grew huge with excitement, almost as round and mad-looking as those of the peacocks staring unbelievingly down at the conversation.

'How did one get here?'

'An ancestor of Lettice and Henry's went on a kind of educational trip to Europe in the 1700s and bought the violin in Italy. Then he had it painted on the door because it was a fashionable thing to do at the time.'

'How did it get lost, the real violin?'

Megan rolled her eyes in exasperation. 'It was Lettice's fault. After she heard Paganini play it she hid it. She said no one else was fit to touch it because it had been played by the maestro. It hasn't been seen since.'

'Alyson said the violin's still here. She said I could find it if you helped me.' Brand's bravado animated the whole of his face.

Megan didn't dare make fun of the suggestion even

though it was ridiculous. Alyson must have meant it as a joke. Megan tried to sound as if she was taking the idea seriously: 'If you're going to find it, we need to do some detective work. I suppose we'll have to talk to Brian Walmsley, seeing as he knows everything there is to know about this place.'

Dad's burly figure burst into the study. 'I've finished! What was it you wanted to see me about?'

Megan passed the pamphlet to Dad, and explained. She tried to ignore the hope blooming in his face. Brand only wanted to find the Guarneri; he hadn't said he wanted to start playing again.

Dad ushered Megan and Brand into the kitchen. When they were settled at the table he rang Brian Walmsley. To Megan's horror she heard Dad invite him for dinner: '...nothing special... we wanted to hear more about the history of The House ... the connection with Paganini ... you seemed the right person to ask.'

Megan almost expected to hear sounds of satisfaction come purring from the phone.

'Fine ... tomorrow ... seven for seven-thirty then ... Bye Brian.'

She left her father and brother to it. They could talk about Paganini and the violin if they wanted; she was more interested in Lettice and Henry and Judith, the witch of Stretton Magna.

In the study she opened the fat books. There were only a few facts embedded in pages and pages of old-fashioned, long-winded English. Megan jotted them down and read on doggedly.

The light dimmed.

Megan yawned and rubbed her eyes as she glanced at the darkening sky.

The curtains at the window stirred.

Someone stood there, half-hidden by thick fabric. Someone watching her.

A whimper quivered in Megan's throat. She jumped up, ran to the light switch, snapped it on. Turned.

There was no one there.

The man-shape was only late afternoon shadows falling over sinuous patterns on the curtain and a draught, pushing through the old window frame, had made them sway.

Megan forced herself to walk calmly across to the window while the peacocks sneered in the failing light. She pulled the curtains closed.

The peacocks were right.

The apparition had been conjured up from nothing more than shapes and shadows, a breeze and tired eyes.

Two Wishes

Muffled shouting from behind the wallpaper thicket invaded Megan's dreamless sleep.

'I'm coming Brand,' she mumbled and pushed aside her duvet.

She sat crouched for a moment at the end of the bed, shivering and only half-awake.

The shouting stopped.

More than anything Megan wanted to stay in her warm bed and fall back to sleep. Instead she dragged her sweat-shirt on and shivered her way to Brand's room.

Her little brother was sitting up, rubbing his fists against his eyes.

She perched beside him. 'What's the matter? Had a bad dream?'

Brand yawned. 'Sort of.'

It hadn't been a nightmare then.

'What did you dream about?'

'There was an old man. I told him to go away. He wouldn't. He got closer and closer and I shouted at him.'

'Sounds scary.'

Brand yawned again. 'Only a bit. He was trying to stop me doing something and it made me angry.'

'What did he want you to stop doing?'

Brand's face scrunched up with the effort of trying to recall his fading dream. 'I can't remember.'

'What was he like, this old man?'

'Tall, thin, pointy nose, white straggly hair. A bogey-man.' Brand made his fingers into talons and waggled them at Megan.

They both laughed.

'If you're not scared I'm going back to bed.' Megan kissed Brand, settled his duvet round him and hurried back to her room. It was so cold she dived into bed without taking her sweatshirt off. But it wasn't only the cold raising goose bumps on her skin. Brand's description of the old man in his dream matched Dad's revenant feature for feature. Megan didn't understand how that could be. She was sure Brand hadn't seen the drawing; he'd been doing his assignment or watching TV while Dad worked.

And Brand's dream had made Megan remember something else, the old man she'd seen reflected in the window on the night they arrived at The House. Common sense had told her then that it was only Brand's reflection twisted by a fault in the glass. Now she wasn't so sure.

She turned over and burrowed deeper. She was being silly. It was The House's fault; lots of things in it weren't exactly what they seemed. If you looked at them full on they were one thing but if you looked sideways they seemed quite different.

She tugged the duvet tightly round herself. She wouldn't think about the old man any more. She'd fill her head with French verbs — that would drive him from her mind and help her get to sleep. At school, grammar always made her want to drift off. It worked. She was asleep in no time, falling into a dream of her own.

Someone was playing a violin in the ballroom. The tune was sweet and Megan almost recognised it. She glided in on noiseless feet. Of course, it was Brand, his swaying figure lit by hundreds and hundreds of candles, their flames flickering in time to the tempo of his playing.

Megan drifted closer.

The melody was simple, haunting. It made her want to dance. She lifted her arms ready to begin.

'Dance with me,' said a voice as cold as death.

A cold, cold hand grasped her wrist.

'Dance with me,' the revenant said again.

'No. I don't want to. I don't want to dance with you.' Megan shrank back.

The revenant clung on. 'Dance with me.' His voice filled Megan's veins with ice like a wind from the north.

'I don't want to!'

She pulled and pulled, moved inch by inch towards the door. But the revenant came with her, his bony hand a shackle binding his dead weight to her.

All the time Brand played on oblivious to everything but his music. Around the ballroom lights were dying. Each time the revenant demanded, 'Dance with me,' another bank of candles went out.

Shadows filled the empty spaces.

The last candle guttered in its sconce lighting the revenant's long, wild hair into a nimbus of icy fingers.

'Dance with me,' he said.

'No!' Megan cried, her shriek in tune with the single, long discordant note Brand drew from the violin.

The candle snuffed out and all was blackness.

The trouble with nightmares, Megan thought the next day, was that they didn't fade like dreams: they stayed with you, vivid and alive, for hours after you woke up. The revenant dogged her all day. By the afternoon she couldn't stand his imaginary presence any longer. She had to get out of The House and away by herself, away from the brooding, mocking atmosphere that had seemed so harmlessly ridiculous at first

If she told Brand she was going for a walk he'd want to go with her and Dad would expect her to agree. She left a note on the kitchen table and slipped away into the woods on her own.

At first her deceit made her feel guilty. She gnawed at her lip, imagining crisis after crisis, Brand needing her, Dad needing her. She shouldn't simply run away like this and leave them to it.

Leave them to what? Nothing they couldn't manage by themselves.

Anger flashed through her, fierce as pain. She had a right to put herself first.

She enjoyed the luxury of hating her father and brother. Then she felt guilty again. Everything was so muddled.

A picture of Mum's face invaded her mind.

'Go away!' Megan ordered. The image stayed: reproachful, infinitely sad. 'Stop it!' Megan pressed her hands to her head as though she could force it out. She wanted to run away from it, from herself, run and run forever.

There was no point. It wouldn't work. Only being with her friends worked and now she was alone and friendless. Dad had seen to that by dumping her in The House in The Hollow with no one to help her escape from remembering what she'd done.

Except, maybe, for Alyson.

She was nice. She cared. She'd helped with the bad foot. It was strange that Brian Walmsley didn't like her. And Dad was getting hostile too. He didn't like Alyson rearranging his drawing materials, or taking Brand to the woods, or giving Megan the remedy. He didn't seem to understand that Alyson wasn't interfering, only trying to be helpful.

Megan didn't see the cat, not until she almost stumbled over it where it sat in the middle of the path, a velvety blot on the autumn leaves. 'Pywackett! What are you doing here?'

Megan realised she was almost at Alyson's cottage by the river. It might be good to talk to her — but did she know her well enough? Pywackett stood up, and Megan began to follow. After all, where else could she go?

Maybe into the forest? She didn't feel confident about that: she might get lost. Doubtfully she peered into the trees.

A face looked back at her. It grinned. It was Robin.

'I knew you'd come back,' Robin said, pushing branches out of the way with one hand. The other held a plastic bag with a head-shaped lump in it.

'I haven't come to help with the bonfire,' Megan said hastily. 'I've come for a walk, to think.'

Robin skipped down on to the path. 'What about?'

'Private things. Problems.' It was a pity Robin was a bit too young to become a proper friend, even a temporary one. Still, she was interesting and it was good to have somebody to talk to. 'What are *you* doing here?' Megan asked.

'I've been mushrooming. D'you want to walk with me?'

Megan couldn't think why not. 'All right'.

They set off into the forest, Robin as sure-footed and confident as Megan was hesitant.

'Doesn't your dad mind you being on your own in the woods?' Megan asked.

'No.'

Megan wasn't sure she believed her. She didn't know if Robin was a typical country child. She was a bit odd, well, different anyway, with her abrupt ways and old-fashioned style of dressing. Her clothes didn't quite fit either: they looked as if they'd been chosen at random by someone who didn't know her size. Perhaps she didn't have a mother to help either. But Megan could hardly ask. Instead she said, 'Have you found any? Mushrooms I mean?'

Robin opened her bag. 'Look.'

The head-shape turned out to be a yellow lump, like a distorted cushion.

'What is it?'

'Chicken of the woods.'

'That's not a chicken!'

'No,' Robin explained patiently, 'it's a fungus and it grows on trees. Posh restaurants pay loads for them, and for chanterelles.' She delved into the bag and pulled out a frilly, pinkish mushroom. 'You have to be careful with these, you can get them mixed up with a poisonous species, *cortinarius speciossimus.*' She sounded as if she knew what she was talking about.

'You learn some funny things in your school,' Megan said.

'I don't go to school.' Robin put the chanterelle back and closed her bag. 'Dad and me live in a collective — that's lots of people living together and sharing everything,' she explained kindly as if Megan couldn't be expected to work out what a collective was for herself. 'We do lessons at home.'

'Where's home?'

'At the edge of Stretton Magna, near the woods, in a big old house.'

'Like The House in The Hollow.'

'No it's not. It's a farmhouse, for one thing, with animals and hens and geese, and it's not haunted, for another.'

Megan's clumsy city feet stumbled, tangled up in undergrowth. She bent to pull it away. 'There's no such thing as ghosts.'

'There is in The House, everybody in Stretton knows.'

Like the taxi driver?

'What sort of ghost?' Megan asked sarcastically, 'a headless monk? A lady in grey?'

'It's an old man. Lots of people have seen him.'

Megan yanked at a strand of ivy winding its twisted fingers round her ankle. 'Like who?'

'People from Stretton.' Robin was less sure of herself now.

Megan tore the ivy away and threw it into the bushes. 'So nobody you actually know has seen it then? It's just a story, a superstition.' She willed Robin to admit it.

She did, in a way. 'My Dad says ghosts are part of folk-memories,' she said defiantly, 'the same as legends and customs, and you ought to respect things from the past and learn from them.'

Megan could think of quite a few things from the past that didn't deserve respect — burning witches for one. 'It's still superstition,' she insisted.

'No it isn't!' Robin tossed her braids in annoyance and stamped off.

'Wait a minute!'

Megan hadn't meant to rubbish Robin's beliefs; she'd only been so adamant because she wanted to convince herself that there couldn't possibly be a ghost haunting The House.

She hurried after Robin. 'I said wait. I'm sorry.'

How had she managed to get that far ahead so fast? The ribbons in her braids flashed a momentary red then she was gone.

Megan turned a slow circle. 'Robin!' The forest grew featureless all around, the path somehow losing itself in drifts of fallen leaves. 'Robin, where are you?'

A coarse crowing answered her. The slow thud of methodical wings passed overhead. A large bird sailed darkly under the canopy of leaves.

Megan moved quickly towards a gap the raven had flown through. On the other side a pathway led leftwards. Megan followed it walking fast. The track led straight to the familiar field of bracken now with the bonfire rising a couple of metres from the neatly cleared circle at its centre.

Robin stood under the wishing tree. 'Nice to see you again,' she grinned as Megan walked up to her.

'Why did you go off like that?' Megan asked furiously.

'It was a good laugh.'

'I don't think it was very funny. I don't know the woods like you. I could've been wandering around for days — well, hours. I wouldn't take you to the city and dump you in the back streets!'

'You're all right aren't you?' Robin said.

'Yes.' All at once Megan felt stupid for making a fuss. Nobody could get lost in an English wood; they weren't big enough, not like in the past. 'I'd better get back,' she said.

'D'you want me to walk you?' Robin asked.

'No thanks!'

'Sure?'

'Positive.'

'Wait a bit.' Robin unbraided one of her plaits and tugged a couple of ribbons free. She held them out to Megan. 'These are for you, to make wishes.'

Megan didn't want to risk offending Robin a second time. She took the silky strips. 'Right. Thanks.'

''S all right Bye.'

Before Megan had time to do more than raise her hand in a wave Robin was gone and Megan was left standing under the wishing tree, looking at the two crimson ribbons spilling from her fingers.

Wishes fluttered in the branches above her.

'Why not?' she said.

She looped the ribbons loosely round her wrist and circled the tree looking for a promising place to climb. She slid her foot on a bunched whorl a few centimetres above the ground. Her fingers grasped two more knots higher up.

Cautiously she levered herself up. She reached the first branch and sat astride it then leaned back, squinting upwards. Rags and ribbons in every shade of red trembled slightly like hundreds of butterflies basking in the sun.

Megan fingered the scarlet slips on her wrist Perhaps wishes were more likely to be answered if they were hard-earned: the more effort you put in, the greater the reward.

The next branch up looked achievable and it still had some twigs bare of blossom. Megan worked herself into a standing position, holding tightly to the second branch and hoping nothing alive was going to move under her fingers. She looked down. The ground swirled.

She concentrated on negotiating hand and footholds. 'Made it.'

She sat carefully on the branch, locking her feet under it, and pulled a ribbon loose. Twisting forward slightly and gripping furiously with her knees, she tied the ribbon to the nearest twig.

How do I make this wish? she puzzled. In my head? Out loud? To the tree?

Glad no one could see her, Megan turned her face to the trunk. She whispered into its flaking, pungent skin, 'I wish I could see my mother again — just once — and tell her I'm sorry I didn't keep my promise.'

She listened to the tree's small sounds — its rustlings and whisperings — and realised she'd been hoping for a miracle.

'Waste of time,' she said bitterly. Making wishes was babyish and futile. She was never going to see her mother again, never. She slapped the trunk hard, hard enough to hurt. The second ribbon fluttered at her wrist. 'It's not worth it,' she muttered.

Still, now she was here ...

She knotted the ribbon on to another twig.

What else could she wish for?

A thought came unbidden.

'I wish I knew who the ghost in The House was.'

The tree shuddered violently, from root to crown. Megan fell into the fork between bough and trunk. She clung on desperately.

Branches thrashed back and forth, leaves cascaded into the air.

The tree screamed, cried out as it beat the air with its branches. Megan felt its torment through her fingers, her knees, her scrabbling feet, and almost saw its pain, streaming like flames from every branch and twig and toppling leaf.

Doorways

Determinedly Megan scanned the facts she'd excavated from the fat books last night and then she tried the books themselves again, in case she'd missed something. There was no mention of the wishing tree or a ghost in The House, just dry pieces of information like dates of construction. She'd have to find her own explanation for why the tree had behaved as it did.

Although the tremor had lasted only a few seconds it had been so violent and the scream so terrible that Megan had been convinced that the roots were being torn from the earth and the tree was about to crash to the ground.

Afterwards she'd clung to the trunk for what seemed like hours listening to the soothing susurration of leaves in the gentle wind. Eventually the chill of dusk forced her to climb down and race back to The House against the coming night. She'd reached it first — just.

Jangle — jangle. The doorbell made her jump.

Brian Walmsley had arrived to tell them all about Paganini and the violin. Dad could let him in.

Megan went to the kitchen where Alyson was busy preparing dinner. She'd already laid out the table with a small posy of wild flowers and herbs by each setting.

'They look pretty,' Megan said.

Alyson favoured Megan with one of her warmly enveloping smiles. 'The tussie mussies? The scent's intended to soothe digestion and induce a mood of contentment.'

Megan sniffed hungrily at a dish giving out a strong, spicy smell. 'What's that?'

'Wild mushrooms, garlic and herbs.'

Megan leaned closer to the pan. 'What sort of mush-rooms are they?'

'Chanterelles. Specially good ones I find on the roots of old trees.'

The others came in. Brain Walmsley clasped his hands together as though they'd escape if he didn't keep them under control. 'Sorry I'm a bit late, somehow time just slipped away.' His hands liberated themselves and flew apart.

'No problem,' Dad said.

Megan didn't know how Dad stood it.

He turned to the housekeeper. 'Thanks for staying late, Alyson. I'm sure you'd like to be off now.'

Megan blushed at Dad's abruptness.

Alyson fetched her coat from the utility room.

'I hope you enjoy your dinner,' she said to Brian Walmsley. 'I've done all your favourites.'

Brian Walmsley's mouth ravelled up into a tight smile.

Megan's eyes went from Alyson to Brian Walmsley to Dad and back to Alyson. She was baffled by the unpleasant atmosphere. She could understand Dad's rudeness even if it was a bit childish — she knew only too well how he hated Alyson moving things in his studio and taking charge of her and Brand without asking first — but she had no idea why Brian Walmsley was so hostile.

In defiance of Dad Megan walked Alyson to the front door wondering how the housekeeper knew what Brian Walmsley's favourite foods were.

Alyson said a warm, 'Goodnight,' at the door. She was such a nice, friendly person, and a really good cook. Even Brand overcame his suspicion of fancy food and finished off the meal.

Megan enjoyed the dinner too though she didn't try the wild mushrooms. Too much garlic, she told herself, which wasn't true: she simply couldn't forget Robin's warning about the poisonous *cortinarius speciossimus* getting mixed up with chanterelles.

After the meal they cleared the table and sat round it to listen to Brian Walmsley tell the story of the Devonports, Niccolò Paganini and the Guarneri Del Gesù violin. How Henry, always a gloomy soul, had withdrawn to The House after his wife's death, never remarrying, indulging every whim of his wilful, clever daughter; turning The House into a Gothic fantasy, creating a ballroom and holding dances and parties for Lettice.

'So,' Brian Walmsley continued, 'when Lettice, like half of the rest of Britain, fell under Paganini's spell, Henry used the Guarneri to tempt him to give a concert at The House. Paganini couldn't resist the offer and, when he played, the audience sat entranced by the exquisite music he coaxed from the violin. Afterwards he praised its beautiful sound and placed it in Lettice's hands, making her promise always to safeguard it for him.

'Lettice took him literally. A few days later, when Henry asked where the Guarneri was, Lettice would only say it was somewhere safe, hidden until the maestro needed it again. No matter how Henry protested Lettice refused to give way.'

'That's stupid!' Brand was bewildered.

Megan wasn't. She and some of her friends had had a big thing about a student teacher last term. Megan managed to get his copy of *Romeo and Juliet* at the end of a lesson and put hers in its place. She took the book home and hid it. The student had to go back to university without it. He lost a textbook and with it all the careful notes he'd written inside; Megan had a piece of him to keep for ever. And her friends' envy when they knew what she'd done almost made up for the guilt she felt at stealing his book. Lettice's reason for hiding the Guarneri didn't seem crazy once you understood the way she thought.

'The real tragedy,' Brian Walmsley said, 'is the double loss of the violin *and* the variation Paganini wrote.'

'What variation?' Megan asked.

Brian Walmsley's smile almost said, Gotcha! 'Apparently he heard someone singing a folk tune, liked it and wrote a variation on it.'

'I'd have thought he'd have made a copy,' Dad said. 'Surely he was too hard-headed a business man to lose a potential money-spinner like a new composition.'

'Ah, yes, except that he didn't lose it He destroyed it.' Brian Walmsley paused for effect.

Get on with it, Megan thought, and stop showing off.

'He played the variation at the Devonports' concert in the ballroom. That night he had a nightmare. He woke his manager with some garbled tale of the tune and a terrifying old man ordering him never to play it again.'

A 'terrifying old man': like the revenant in her own nightmare? and the one in Brand's dream? Megan sneaked a look at her little brother. All his attention was on Brian Walmsley.

'The manager tried to convince Paganini that he'd simply had a bad dream. Paganini flew into one of the rages he was famous for and threw the composition into the fire in his room.'

'Do you think the violin's still here?' Brand asked.

Brian Walmsley leaned towards him across the table. 'Absolutely. Every time we carry out renovations I do another search. Unfortunately — so far — nothing. But I'm certain it's here.'

He leaned even closer and lowered his voice: 'Perhaps you'll have better luck. If you do, let me know.'

Dad ruffled Brand's hair. 'No unauthorised searches. Come and ask permission before you go poking around.'

'OK,' Brand said.

Megan stood up. Now she knew the story she'd had enough of Brian Walmsley. 'I'm going upstairs.'

'It's early.' Dad didn't like her leaving while they had a guest. But Dad had been rude to Alyson so why couldn't

74

she be rude to Brian Walmsley? Still, it would save trouble if she could think up an excuse. 'I need to catch up on my reading, for the assignment.'

It was a relief to get away from Brian Walmsely: being a good story-teller didn't make him less creepy, only more bearable. He had told her a bit more about Lettice though. She was pleased about that.

She stopped by the library door. This had been Lettice's House, surely there'd be a copy of her book here. Once inside Megan realised she had no idea what sort of book she was looking for. She went to the portrait over the empty fireplace.

'What did you write?' she asked Lettice. 'I bet it was a novel, all eerie and Gothic, like *Frankenstein* or *Dracula*.'

The small red book in Lettice's hand glinted like a ruby against her yellow satin dress. If it was a copy of her own book it was too little to be a novel — all the Victorian ones Megan knew were pretty long.

She turned and ran her eye up and down the shelves. The books were all sizes and colours. At least they'd been sorted into subjects and alphabetical order.

Lettice's book wasn't among the novels, or any of the other subjects Megan tried first. She found it sitting between two thick tomes by Geoffrey Chaucer and John Donne.

Poetry? Lettice wrote poetry!

Megan pulled the book free, surprised at how small and slim the little red leather volume was. Gold lettering on the spine read simply, *Poems* and *Lettice Devonport*.

Megan riffled through creamy pages edged with a stroke of gold. At the front a dedication said: *This book is most humbly dedicated to the inestimable virtuoso, Signor Niccolò Paganini.*

Paganini!

Avidly Megan fanned the pages again. The name 'Paganini' flickered by in one of the long titles Lettice seemed to have liked: *Sublime Perfection: on hearing Signor Paganini play the Devonport Guarneri Del Gesù violin.*

Megan read a few lines.

'It doesn't make any sense,' she told Lettice's portrait.

Fire roared to life in the empty hearth. Yellow flames shot upwards, outwards.

Megan dropped the book.

The noise and light vanished as abruptly as they'd appeared. The House was up to its tricks again, making car headlights seem like flames in the dim light of the library. Brian Walmsley had just swept his car round, turning so sharply that his headlights swirled through the window into the hearth and the tyres roared on the gravel.

'Why did he have to keep frightening her like that?'

She stopped and picked up the book. She'd read it upstairs, in comfort.

Relaxing back in bed after she'd swabbed her foot with the rest of Alyson's remedy, Megan picked up Lettice's book. She found the *Sublime Perfection* poem, and eagerly read it again. It still didn't make any sense. She tried one of the more obscure verses out loud:

> *His muse upon her lyre plays*
> *But no sounds take their flight*
> *For she my dearest wish obeys*
> *And shields the instrument from sight.*

What was a muse? And why did she want to shield her lyre?

There was a knock at the door and Dad put his head round it. 'Brian's gone.'

'I know — good.'

'Do you have to be quite so hostile?' Dad asked, coming in and perching on the bed.

'Yes, he's a sleazoid.'

Dad gave up being the heavy father. He laughed as he read Lettice's name on the spine of the book. 'Any good?'

Megan had to be honest. 'Not really.'

Dad leaned against a carved post. 'Read me a bit.'

Megan turned to the Guarneri poem.

'Oh ho! Clues to the violin's whereabouts,' Dad said.

'I don't think so, listen.'

She read:

No other hand can make it sing
So it must silence keep,
To fly no more on music's wing
But in the darkness softly sleep

Where wheeling stars whirl overhead
And singing spheres rejoice,
Where planets all are music led
And lend to harmony their voice.

'You're right, it's not very good,' Dad said. 'I bet Henry had the book privately printed for Lettice. He spent a fortune indulging that girl. It's no wonder his money went down the tubes and he had to shut up The House and retire to London.'

'Didn't they ever come back?'

Dad shook his head. 'The upkeep was too much, even for Henry. The House was neglected for generations, left to crumble until the last Devonport died and The Sanctuary Trust bought it They help pay for its upkeep by letting it out to people like us who want holidays away from it all.'

'We're not on holiday.'

'We are away from it all.'

'We'll have to go back eventually.'

'Things will be better, eventually.'

'Maybe,' Megan wriggled down into bed.

Dad kissed her forehead. 'Goodnight, angel.'

'Stop it, Dad — I'm not an angel — I'm just Megan.'

'You're an angel with Brand.'

Megan glared.

'All right,' he said. 'Sorry. Goodnight, Megan.'

On the edge of sleep Megan became aware of someone standing at her bedside.

'Go away, Brand,' she mumbled.

Dimly she heard a dull thud and a muffled sliding noise. The figure shambled away.

Tomorrow, Megan decided dreamily. Tomorrow I'll tell him to lock that connecting door.

In the morning, Megan thanked Alyson for the remedy. 'It really worked. My foot's better.'

'What was in it, Alyson?' Dad asked.

'Only an infusion of herbs. Quite harmless.'

'Maybe. I'd still prefer you to ask before prescribing medicines of any kind for my children.'

'Of course. I should have done that.' Although her words were humble, somehow Alyson was not.

Megan didn't like being fought over. She joined Brand in the study.

She managed to finish writing up her notes for the assignment but it wasn't easy: Brand kept pestering her about what Brian Walmsley had told them last night.

Megan put her pen down. 'That's done. D'you want to come and explore the river?' That way she could avoid going near the wishing tree.

'No.' She expected him to say he wanted to go and help Robin. 'I want to find the Guarneri.'

'Just like that!'

'Yes.'

Megan pushed her papers to one side. She couldn't help

thinking that if she somehow got into Lettice's mind and worked out how she thought, it might just be possible to discover where she'd hidden the violin.

'Where do you want to look first?' she asked Brand.

'Upstairs. We haven't been in that other wing yet.'

All the rooms in the east wing were empty and layered with sheets of dust, except for one: that was full of junk. They poked around the empty, uncarpeted rooms first, drumming at the walls, kicking at the skirting boards.

'Nothing up here.' Brand's muffled voice came from the fireplace where he stood with his head and shoulders out of sight up the chimney.

'You don't hide a violin up a chimney,' Megan said, 'not unless you want it to go up in flames. Let's try the junk room.'

She led the way. Stuff piled up the walls and across the room, packed in from floor to ceiling.

Brand tugged at a padded chair. Megan shifted an ornate music stand. Together they hauled a bulky lectern, carved like a bird with outspread wings, away from the wall.

In front of Megan a grey figure moved. Startled, she let go of her side of the lectern with a thump.

'What's the matter?' Brand leaned towards her and a second shadowy figure appeared: two shapes trapped in a round gilt frame. It was a mirror reflecting their images behind its cataract of milky dust.

Megan swept her hand over the glass. Their faces appeared in sharp focus.

Brand coughed in the swirling dust. 'We looked like ghosts!'

Revenants.

Megan nodded. 'It's this House. It makes you think you see spooky things when you don't really.'

They shifted the mirror. Behind it was a portrait painting. The dark face regarded them haughtily.

79

'Dad ought to see this,' Megan said. They pulled the painting clear and propped it by the door frame. Megan left Brand to slide into a narrow gap behind the piled up furniture by the back wall while she studied the painting. All at once she felt trapped between the staring picture and the mirror's cloudy eye.

'I've found something,' Brand called.

Megan squeezed herself behind the heap of furniture to where Brand was pulling at a handle in the wall. A small door opened halfway, partially blocked by a chest of drawers.

'Come on!' Brand, made bold by excitement, went through the doorway.

Megan poked her head into the dark space behind the little door. Brand's feet climbed above her up a spiral, wooden staircase. She followed them into the dark.

The stairs creaked.

A long finger of cobweb tentatively stroked her face. She brushed it away. It fell back and stickily caressed her hair. She stumbled hastily on in the pitch darkness, hands scrabbling at rough, cold walls.

She caught up with Brand. 'I can feel another door,' he said.

Megan heard a rattling sound and daylight suddenly tumbled towards her from the hollow, stone room of a turret. Light and a thin wind entered through four glassless, slitted windows. A whistling sound, too faint and high-pitched to be the wind, came from rafters supporting the pointed roof. Dark clusters of small creatures clung there.

'Bats,' Megan said. 'We'd better not disturb them, they're probably hibernating or something.'

'I want to explore.'

'No point. You couldn't hide a violin in here — too cold and wet in winter.'

It was more difficult going down in the dark than climbing up. Megan put a hand against each wall and stepped cautiously. Halfway down she touched a cold ring.

'Brand!'

'What?'

'I've found another door handle.'

The ring turned smoothly. The small door swung open.

'I know where this is!' Megan said.

Nine Ladies Dancing

Megan and Brand stood on the balcony under the glass dome scattered with its faded gilt stars and ghostly silver moon. Bright sunlight made them look tawdry and rather sad. The same forlorn look shaded the faces of the life-sized figures painted on panels around the gallery.

'I think it's safe.' Megan trod cautiously on to the narrow walkway. Brand followed. They circled the gallery in opposite directions and met up in front of a woman dancing with a lyre in her arms. Brand ran his fingers over the instrument as if music might spring from the painted strings.

'How many ladies are there?' Megan asked hastily.

'One, two...' Brand counted them off. '...nine,' he finished.

A cloud drifted overhead, blotting out the light and tugging shadows over the painted figures.

Dad's voice boomed up from the hall: 'Brand! Megan!'

They pressed back against the wall of the gallery and slid silently along until they reached the door. They slipped through, closed it and went down the stairs to the junk room as quickly as they dared in the darkness then shoved the chest of drawers against the turret door to hide it.

They reached the top of the stairs at the same time as Dad.

'Where've you two been? Lunch's ready.'

'Only exploring. The rooms are all empty,' Brand said innocently.

'Except one, filled with junk,' Megan added before Dad could start demanding to know what they'd been exploring for, as if he hadn't guessed already. 'We found a painting. Come and see.'

Dad couldn't resist that and followed her back to the junk room. He scanned the portrait swiftly and expertly. 'Only a copy, I'd guess, but a good one.' He picked up one side of the picture. 'Give me a hand. I want it in my studio.'

The three of them struggled downstairs and leaned the painting against the wall in front of Dad's drawing board.

'Won't it put you off, him staring at you while you work?' Megan asked. She wasn't sure how she felt about the proud, swarthy face.

'Adds to the atmosphere. I like the forbidding look.'

Dad assessed the picture again. 'You know, I reckon this is a portrait of Paganini. The costume's right for the period and the satanic look fits descriptions I've read of him. Rumour had it he was in league with the devil, which was supposed to explain his phenomenal playing skills.' Dad brushed a finger over the painting. 'You can see how the painter's got something of that slightly threatening mystery and come up with a pretty good version of "Paganini-the-legend".'

'I wonder what the picture's doing in The House,' Megan said.

Dad shrugged. 'It was probably commissioned for Lettice since she was such a fan. I'll ring Brian about it after lunch.'

Megan sighed in exasperation: Brian Walmsley again.

She slipped an arm through Dad's. 'Lettice didn't seem to be scared of him did she? And Henry would never have let anybody really dangerous near his daughter.'

'Very perceptive of them,' Dad said. 'It's a pity Lettice went over the top and hid the Guarneri. Which reminds me — I told you not to go looking for it without getting permission first.'

Megan stopped pretending they hadn't been searching for the violin. 'We didn't find it.'

'I don't think you'll find it conveniently lying about waiting to be found,' Dad said. 'Lettice must've thought up somewhere really devious. And talking of devious,' Dad steered Megan and Brand towards the kitchen, 'you two were supposed to be studying. No more exploring today.'

Brand was a bit absent-minded that afternoon. His pen rolled unnoticed off the table. Megan picked it up. 'What's the matter?'

'I want to play the Guarneri. I want to play that Paganini piece on it, the one I learned with Mum. She'll like that.'

Megan's heart sank: this wasn't fair.

'Even if we find it,' she said, 'I'm not sure you'd be able to play it. For a start you don't know what sort of condition it'd be in. It's been lying around for about a hundred and fifty years, don't forget. Anyway, no one's going to let a little kid play it, it must be worth zillions!'

Brand's face clenched mutinously. 'Alyson said I could!' Sudden tears clung to his eyelashes.

For a moment Megan found herself disliking the housekeeper.

'Oh, come here.' Megan hugged him tight. 'We'll try and find it, we really will. I want to as well you know. But you've got to be patient. Alyson's making it sound dead easy and it's not.'

Alyson shouldn't keep pushing Brand about the Guarneri, it only upset him. Dad would go mad if he knew.

Brand sniffed. His skinny arms loosened. 'When can we start looking again? Now?'

'I said be patient! Plans first. Besides, I want Dad to run me into Stretton so I can post my notes off to school. You can come as well.'

That should give her some time to think. 'Finish what you're doing,' she said, 'and I'll check with Dad.'

She looked tentatively round the studio door. Inside

84

Dad drew, effortlessly, gracefully, lost in the enchanted world of his imagination. Megan tapped lightly against the door frame.

'Come in!' Dad bellowed cheerfully. The work must be going well.

Megan stood by the drawing table. 'Got a storyline yet?'

'Not exactly.' Dad wafted his hand over a sequence of pencil drawings, brief outlines too sketchy to tell Megan much. He pointed to one of them. 'I've indulged myself and polished up this rough.' He put a larger version of it on to the table. It was a courtroom scene with a man pointing at a terrified-looking woman in the dock. The finer detail revealed people in seventeenth-century clothes. Dad must've visited the museum. The drawing was a close rendering of the tableau behind the red curtain. That wasn't like Dad, to copy. She started to ask him about it when something else caught her eye, made her catch her breath.

'That man's like the revenant on your cover.'

Dad slid the title page alongside the courtroom scene. The faces of the accuser and the revenant were definitely the same though the first was younger and filled with fury while the second was filled with despair.

'I don't know how you managed to get him looking like that,' Megan said.

'I used the mirror.' Dad nodded towards the cheval glass he'd brought with him from home. Ever since Megan could remember she'd seen Dad stand in front of it twisted into the poses he wanted to draw. He'd spent hours amusing her and Brand by acting out surprise or laughter or horror, and then making rapid drawings of his reflection. They'd loved it. And loved it still more when they were the subjects and Dad drew them.

Megan shook her head. 'I didn't mean that. I meant the expression. How you got it to look so horrible and real.'

'It's easy. I dig into my feelings and draw what I find there.'

Megan didn't like Dad being on familiar terms with anger and despair, it reminded her too much of how she felt. But he hadn't betrayed Mum like she had.

'I'm sorry to interrupt now, when your work's coming right, but I need to go to Stretton, to post my stuff off to school. Brand wants to come as well. I think he's sorry he didn't go with us yesterday.'

Dad immediately covered his drawings and tidied his materials away. Megan felt a bit mean at deliberately getting him to stop working. It couldn't be helped. She needed him to distract Brand so she had time to think about how to handle the quest for the Guarneri without raising false hopes in Brand.

For once, there was plenty to keep Brand occupied in Stretton: market stalls had sprouted like toadstools in the square. It was obviously the day of the main market.

As soon as Dad parked, Brand was away, poking round piles of bric-a-brac and junk.

'When I've posted these notes I want to go to the museum,' Megan said.

'What for?' Dad asked.

'I need some more information, those books didn't tell me much.'

'See if there's any prints or postcards with seventeenth-century dress while you're there. It's always handy to check on costume details.' Dad pulled out his wallet. 'Don't forget to make a contribution if they're asking for donations. Meet us by the memorial when you've finished.'

Megan went off to the Post Office and bought stamps for her assignment. She jammed the envelope into the letterbox slot.

School would be happy when they got it.

Brand was happy because Megan was going to help him find the violin.

Dad was happy because his work was coming on.

Megan supposed she'd better go and be happy in the museum.

The same attendant sat at the reception desk looking as if he hadn't moved since Megan's last visit.

'Is your witch display working now?' she asked him.

He shook his head. 'Still waiting for the engineer, I'm afraid. Maybe next week.'

He peered closely at Megan from behind his rimless glasses. 'I don't recall you coming in here before.'

'I came a couple of days ago. I'm interested in The House in The Hollow because I'm staying there for a bit. Have you got any books or leaflets?'

He rooted about under his desk and came up with a shallow box filled with cards and a few pamphlets.

'Is there anything on Lettice and Henry Devonport or Paganini?'

The attendant shook his head. 'Sorry, no.'

Megan wasn't surprised about the Devonports, not after what the librarian had told her, but she was about Paganini.

'Wouldn't Paganini be good publicity for Stretton?'

'He would be, if only we could afford to make a splash about him. We used all our budget to set up the witch display. I'd like to make Paganini's connection with Stretton our next project though I doubt we'll be able to afford it. County finances don't stretch far, especially in a backwater like Stretton.'

'Have you got anything about Walter Devonport and Judith Moone?'

The attendant shuffled through the contents of the box. 'I did have some literature but we had a group in yesterday and they bought everything. Legend has it, you know, that on Samhain night Judith haunts the woods where she died.'

'What's Samhain?'

'31 October — Hallowe'en to you and me. But Samhain's

an older festival, much older, from pagan times. On Samhain the doors between this world and the next open and Judith comes searching for her betrayer. And they do say that the goings on in The Hollow get worse around that time too.'

'You mean, there's a ghost in the woods there?'

'The woods? No, not in the woods, not that I've heard. No, no. In the ... here we are. Have a look at these.'

Megan took the wad of cards he held out.

'There's Judith.' He pointed at a card of the print in the annexe. 'And there's Sir Walter, and that's a miniature painting of Phillip Devonport.' The card showed a round picture set into an ornate frame.

'Who's Phillip?'

'The son of Sir Walter Devonport. Judith Moone bewitched him and he died of the falling sickness.'

'How did they know it was Judith?'

'When Phillip fell ill, Jacob Fisher, steward at The House, denounced Judith to Sir Walter. He had her arrested and her house searched. They found one of Phillip's gloves drenched in a foul-smelling liquid and pierced all over with thorns. That was enough evidence. Her fate was sealed.'

Megan paid for two pictures each of the tableau, the witch, and Sir Walter Devonport. On the way out she put a pound of Dad's change in the appeals box knowing the attendant would hear its heavy clunk on the bottom of the empty box. She put in another pound of her own to keep the first one company.

'Every little helps,' she said.

House of Cards

From the steps of the museum Megan had a clear view across the market square. At the memorial cross clustered a small crowd. Dad stood on its fringe next to Brand.

A drum roll tumbled round the square. Bells jingled. A chorus of yells rose from inside the group of watchers.

Morris men. Megan pulled a face as she threaded her way between the stalls towards the cross.

Another yell. A fiddle struck up a tune. An accordion joined in.

"Scuse me,' Megan said to the back of a tall woman blocking her path on the edge of the crowd.

The woman turned. 'Certainly.'

'Oh, hello,' Megan said as Alyson made way for her.

Megan wriggled in between Dad and Brand. 'Didn't think this was your kind of thing,' she teased Brand.

He was puzzled. 'It's music,' he said indignantly, as if that explained everything.

'Don't you think folk music's interesting?' Dad grinned.

Megan shrugged: with the crowd of townspeople around her she wasn't quite brave enough to say she thought it horrible. 'You know I'm not musical, not like Brand.' And that's the understatement of the year, she thought. Music was a foreign language she could never hope to learn and musicians were magicians.

The morris men jumped high in the air, flourishing red handkerchiefs and whooping loudly. Stamping and shaking ankle bells they danced backwards and forwards, driving a man dressed as a fool in a ragged orange and yellow costume round and round.

A final yell, a final leap and the dancers closed in on the Fool.

The crowd clapped, the morris men bowed and the raggedy man held out his horned cap. 'Come on, ladies and gents, drop in a few coins for The Men of Stretton.' He whacked Brand on the head with a red balloon tied to a stick.

'Here,' Dad handed Brand some loose change. 'For good luck.'

The coins chimed in the cap.

The musicians struck up a new tune. The men formed another dance and some kind of leafy circlet flew from dancer to dancer. Two young women began to laugh and nudge each other. One let out a piercing wolf-whistle as the lead dancer whirled the circlet above his head.

'Can we go now?' Megan asked Dad.

'If you want.'

Brand kept his attention on the dancers. 'I like this tune. I want to stay.'

Dad hesitated.

'Come on,' Megan urged. She didn't like the morris dancing: grown men leaping about in silly clothes.

Alyson spoke from beside her: 'Why don't you stay and watch this dance to the end?' The housekeeper's eyes were half-closed and her head was tipped slightly to one side as she listened to the fiddle and the drum. 'It won't take long. You'll find it interesting if only you'll let yourself listen carefully.'

'OK, home,' Dad said.

Oh right, Megan thought, now you're deciding to go because Alyson wants me to stay.

'I wish I could go home, back to my real home,' she murmured. She hadn't meant Dad to hear but he did.

'You know that's impossible,' he said softly. His face took on the sad, resigned look that always redoubled Megan's guilt.

She walked to the car and leaned against it. Dad stayed with Brand.

Megan's foot tapped in time to the insistent music. She found herself humming the tune. It sounded familiar. She listened carefully. She *did* know it from somewhere. The dance ended and the music stopped. The melody began to fade from Megan's mind. If only she could hold on to it long enough to remember where she'd heard it before. It was no use, she couldn't. In moments it was gone.

Back at The House Brian Walmsley waited, relaxed in his immaculate red car.

'I want a private word with Brian,' Dad said unlocking the front door. 'Can you kids get us some tea?' He led Brian Walmsley into his studio.

'I get the feeling they want us out of the way,' Megan said to Brand as they clattered around the vast kitchen. 'I wonder what they're talking about.'

'Boring stuff.'

'Maybe. Maybe not.' Dad had looked a bit grim. He'd seemed all right on the way back, though, joking with Brand about the morris men and the wolf-whistling women.

Megan pushed some packets of biscuits and a big plate in Brand's direction. 'Here. Arrange these. I'll go and tell them it's ready.'

'You just want to stick your nose in,' Brand said.

'Bet you can't build a tower out of those biscuits.'

'Dad'll say it's wasteful.'

'He'll think you're being creative.'

'I'll make the leaning tower of Pisa.'

Megan left Brand setting out a foundation of fig rolls and Garibaldi biscuits. It ought to keep him busy for a bit.

The door to the studio was open. Brian Walmsley lounged against Dad's prized drawing table. 'Are you sure it was her?' he asked Dad.

Megan stood quite still in the doorway. She wanted to know who 'her' was.

'Of course I am. The kids know better than to touch anything of mine and there's no one else in The House except her. Unless,' Dad added sarcastically, 'we've got ghosts.'

'D'you believe in ghosts?'

'Is that a serious question?'

For once Brian Walmsley didn't grin. 'Nothing's been damaged has it?'

'That's not the point Alyson's moved my work around and quite systematically too, as if she's been sorting through it, trying to see what I'm doing. When I tackled her about it she gave me some story about "protecting" the studio from something or other. The only thing it needs protecting from is her. It's not good enough, Brian, you've got to stop her. I know it's difficult in view of your past relationship but in this situation you're her employer before you're anything else and you've got to get her sorted.'

Before Megan could overhear any more Brian Walmsley caught sight of her in the doorway. His smile sprang to attention.

Megan tried not to look as if she'd been eavesdropping. 'Your tea's ready,' she said brightly.

'Brian dropped by to tell us about the Paganini portrait,' Dad explained.

Megan moved next to Dad so he was between her and Brian Walmsley.

'I thought he'd told you earlier, on the phone?' she said.

'Not in detail,' Brian Walmsley said. 'Just that Mike guessed right; it is a portrait of Paganini. One of these days I'll get around to hanging it somewhere appropriate, till then your father's welcome to keep it in here. It's not valuable, only a copy.'

The three of them looked at Paganini. Dark eyes set in a gaunt, aloof face gazed back.

Brian Walmsley went on, 'Henry commissioned the copy for Lettice. It's a typical example of her enthusiasm for Paganini. Like hiding the Guarneri.'

'Or writing that awful poem about him. The one you read to me, Megan,' Dad added.

'It wasn't that bad.'

Brain Walmsley shot a glance at Dad. 'Poetry's a very adolescent thing, don't you think, Mike? Just right for hero worship.'

For one horrible moment Megan thought Dad was going to agree and that the two of them were going to become allies in ridiculing her and Lettice. Instead he said, 'I wouldn't call Shakespeare "adolescent".'

'And I wouldn't call Lettice Shakespeare,' Brian Walmsley countered, 'not on the evidence of the bit of her writing I managed to get through.'

'I never said she was a genius,' Megan said. 'You could try reading more of her work. You might appreciate it then. It's got something.'

She stormed out wishing she hadn't stood up for Lettice's poems when she knew perfectly well they were no good. She hadn't been able to stop herself: Brian Walmsley was so condescending and Lettice didn't deserve that. You probably had to read her poetry two or three times before you understood it. Megan bet herself that Brian Walmsley hadn't got beyond the first page. Even she had only read it through once. She'd try again.

In her room Megan couldn't see Lettice's book. It took some time before she found it under one of the fat chairs, behind a lion's paw. She turned the book over, inspecting its red covers. At least it wasn't marked. She plumped up her pillows, collapsed back into them and read the poems again willing them to be even a little bit better than she remembered. Doggedly she read from cover to cover going over the Paganini poem three times. When she got to the end she dropped the postcards she'd forgotten to give Dad into the book and snapped it shut.

Brian Walmsley was right. The poems were terrible.

She leaned over and put the book into a drawer in the bedside table. She reached for the little gilt key in its lock then hesitated.

No one but her was interested in Lettice's poetry. On the other hand, how the book had found its way under the lion's paw was a mystery. Feeling foolish Megan turned the key. She felt even sillier next morning when she unlocked the drawer and took the postcards out of the book to take to Dad. She deliberately left the key unturned in its drawer as she went down to the kitchen.

'What's that?' Brand asked eyeing Megan's little pile of cards.

'Costume reference for Dad.'

She pushed the cards over to Brand. He laid them out in a row. 'The witch's dead scary!'

Alyson sat herself opposite him. 'Judith was young and beautiful, this is just propaganda.'

Brand laughed. 'The giant cat's got the same name as yours, Pywackett.'

'I told you, it's a traditional name.'

'Good job we don't believe in witches any more,' Megan said.

'Don't we?' the housekeeper said.

'No, not nowadays.'

Alyson picked up the card. 'Judith was housekeeper here, in The House.'

'Like you,' Brand said.

'Yes, like me.' Alyson put the card down again.

Megan gathered them all up. 'I'm taking these to Dad,' she said.

Dad liked the portraits. 'Excellent. Plenty of detail.' He clipped the pictures along the top of his board.

Megan put the card of the courtroom tableau next to the

portraits. Dad's face was a study in astonishment. He reached into the portfolio propped against the side of the table, took out his courtroom drawing and laid it on the board.

The tableau and the drawing weren't just similar, they were identical: the same number of onlookers were in the same positions in the same room with the same layout, the same furnishings. Judith Moone's stance and expression were the same and so were her accuser's.

'Well.' Dad leaned back in his chair. 'I always knew I had a magpie memory but I've absolutely no recollection of storing this away.'

'I don't understand,' Megan said.

'I only have to look at a thing once and it's there in my mental files. I swear I can always recall my sources, but this time ...' Dad shook his head. 'I haven't a clue where I've seen this before.'

'It's in Stretton museum.'

'I've never been there.'

'You must've. When you showed me this drawing before I thought you'd done it that way on purpose.'

'You know I never copy: take bits and pieces, styles, techniques and so on, yes — copy outright, no way,' Dad rapped a pencil at the card in disgust. 'I must've seen it in a book somewhere and forgotten. No wonder it all came so easily to me.' He threw the pencil down.

'Where did you get the idea for your story in the first place?'

Dad shifted uncomfortably. 'Alyson. I went into the woods the day after I arrived here and stopped to draw her cottage. She came out and we got chatting. She told me about a local legend saying one of her ancestors, who'd lived in the cottage in the seventeenth century, had been burned as a witch.'

An ancestor. No wonder Alyson knew so much about Judith and wanted to stand up for her.

'I can't use the drawing now,' Dad said. 'Pity, I'd just started making notes for the colourist. Would you believe, scarlet for the dress.'

Petulantly he snatched at the illustration.

For a moment Megan was afraid he was going to crumple the picture up and throw it away. Instead he pinned it on the far wall beside Paganini's portrait. Then he fixed the postcards above it. 'I'll have to start thinking up a new spin on the storyline. It won't matter about the portraits, they're history and up for grabs, it's just the court scene. I'll have to come at it from another angle. Heaven knows what though. The muse has deserted me.'

A line from Lettice's Paganini poem scrolled through Megan's mind: 'His muse upon her lyre plays'. 'What exactly is a muse?'

'A sort of goddess who inspires you to work. You blame drying up on your muse clearing off. I won't bother making excuses. I'm going out because I'm fed up at the thought of having to make new drawings for a scene I thought I'd finished.' He ushered Megan through the door. 'Anyway, I think only writers and musicians have muses, not artists. I'm certain there isn't one for graphic novelists.'

Dad guessed right, there wasn't a muse for painters. Megan discovered that when she went to the monkey library and looked them up in an ancient encyclopaedia. She wrote down all nine of their names and which art each one represented. Then she took out Lettice's book and read her inscrutable Paganini poem again. She'd been right! Understanding Lettice *was* the key to discovering where she'd hidden the violin. The solution was like a cryptic crossword — perfectly clear once the penny dropped — and Lettice had left Megan all the clues she needed.

The Music of the Spheres

'I know where Lettice hid the Guarneri.'

For a moment Brand was shocked into stillness then he sprang from his chair in the TV room like a jack-in-the-box. 'Where is it? Where's the violin?' Megan laughed: Brand wanted action, not explanations. She couldn't resist making him listen to how clever she'd been though. 'Sit down again and I'll tell you.'

She pulled up a chair and placed the red book between them on the table. 'The answer was in this book of Lettice's all the time. Brian Walmsley wouldn't have missed it if he hadn't been too snotty to read her poetry; she practically gave instructions about where to find the violin. The trouble was, her poetry's not very good so I don't think many people actually read it.'

Not even Megan would have read it again so carefully if she hadn't been sure that once Lettice had stopped adoring Paganini she must have wanted to put right what she'd done. Like Megan had with the student's book. In the end she'd told her form tutor that she'd taken it by mistake and asked him to return it for her. Lettice, though, probably didn't want to lose face and give in to Henry's demands to tell him what she'd done with the Guarneri. Instead she devised this complicated puzzle for people to unravel.

Megan read out the title: '"*Sublime Perfection: on hearing Signor Paganini play the Devonport Guarneri Del Gesù violin.*"' She glanced out of the corner of her eye. Brand's face was grave and full of hope.

She went on, 'The first bit describes Paganini's playing: lots of stuff about how no one else could ever hope to be as

97

good as him or play the Guarneri so well. Then you get three really strange verses. Listen to the first two.'

Megan read slowly, hoping the poems still made sense to her.

> *No other hand can make it sing*
> *So it must silence keep*
> *To fly no more on music's wing*
> *But in the darkness softly sleep*

> *Where wheeling stars whirl overhead*
> *And singing spheres rejoice,*
> *Where planets all are music led*
> *And lend to harmony their voice.*

'I think the first verse tells us Lettice has decided to hide the violin "in the darkness" because nobody else can "make it sing" like Paganini.'

Brand nodded solemnly. Megan knew how hard he was longing for her to be right. 'The other verse shows us roughly where she hid it. The stars and planets are supposed to be an image of music.' Megan looked up from the book. 'Brand, where in The House have we got planets and stars?'

'The dome! The violin's in the dome!'

'I think Lettice tells us exactly *where* in the dome.'

She read out the last verse.

> *His muse upon her lyre plays*
> *Though no sounds take their flight*
> *For she my dearest wish obeys*
> *And shields the instrument from sight.*

'Dad sort of joked that his muse had deserted him because he couldn't work any more and that gave me a clue.' Megan pulled out the list of muses she'd written down and tucked into the back of the book. 'Those women in long frocks dancing round the dome are muses.' She ran her finger down the list. 'The muse of Music is Euterpe, and guess what? She's often painted playing a lyre.'

Megan tapped the book. '"His muse upon her lyre plays", that's Paganini's muse inspiring his playing. "Though no sounds take their flight." Why not? Because Euterpe's "obeying" Lettice's "dearest wish" and "shielding" the Guarneri "from sight". The violin's got to be hidden behind that picture of Euterpe in the painted gallery under the dome of stars.'

Brand's face radiated delight. He leaped up and hugged Megan so fiercely she dropped the book.

She wriggled free, picked it up and dusted it down anxiously. 'Be careful, Brand. Brian Walmsley'll go mad if we damage it!'

Brand ignored her. 'Let's go and tell Dad now!'

Doubt, like a stone, settled in Megan's heart. She might have put that radiant look on Brand's face by offering him a false hope. 'The Guarneri might not be there,' she warned.

'It will be.'

'Anyway, you can't tell Dad at the moment. He's gone out, hasn't he?'

Brand's face fell. 'I forgot.'

Megan slipped an arm round Brand's shoulders. 'You can tell him when he gets back. I bet he won't be long.'

***

Megan was wrong. Alyson told them Dad had phoned to the mobile he'd left at The House and said he wouldn't be back until late. Alyson had promised to stay till then.

'It's not fair,' Brand protested. 'I've got something really important to tell him. I want to talk to him now.'

Alyson gently stroked his silky hair. 'You can tell me.'

'No,' said Megan, 'It's something Brand has to tell Dad

first. Then he can tell everybody else. That's right, isn't it, Brand?'

Brand sighed noisily: 'Yeah, I suppose so.'

Alyson lifted her hand from his head. 'In that case, why don't you go and watch TV.' She dismissed them with one of her enchanting smiles.

Brand hurled himself noisily on the sofa. 'I hope Dad gets back before I go to bed. I want to tell him. I want to go and get the violin.'

'Not tonight! Dad'll have to tell Brian Walmsley first and I bet he'll have to get permission from The Sanctuary Trust before he goes tearing up The House.'

Brand scrunched himself up into a sulky ball in one corner of the sofa.

Megan switched on the TV. Cartoon figures reeled jerkily across the screen. 'Promise you won't tell Alyson before you tell Dad.'

'Only if *you* promise *you* won't tell him if you're still up when he gets back.'

'It's a deal. Now I'm going to do some more work.'

'Boff.' Brand, almost swallowed by the bulging sofa, watched a dinosaur burp a crimson cloud out of the side of its mouth.

Megan left him watching.

'Megan. Megan. Wake up!' Brand was shaking her shoulder. 'Wake up. It's me.'

She struggled into a sitting position. 'What's the matter? Are you all right?'

'I can't sleep. I've decided. Let's go and get the Guarneri.'

Megan was too tired to laugh. 'Don't be silly, Brand. What's the time?'

'I'm not being silly. I think it's about four.' Megan felt the bed give as Brand climbed aboard. 'We've got to get the violin ourselves — you said nobody would let me play it because it's worth millions and millions and I'm only a little kid — I bet Dad won't let me look for it — I bet he'll tell Mr Walmsley and he'll take over and we won't be allowed to do the discovering — I bet they won't even let us watch them look ...' He had to stop babbling to take a breath.

Megan tried to think straight. She forced her mind to run through Brand's arguments. They did make sense: as soon as Dad and Brian Walmsley had the information they'd start organising everything. She'd done all the work: read Lettice's awful poetry, learned how her mind worked, made the connection with the muses and deciphered the cryptic poem. Brian Walmsley didn't deserve to get all the glory, she did. 'We'll do it.'

She slid out of bed and pulled on her jeans and sweatshirt. 'We'll need tools.'

'There's some in the utility room. Where all the spare light bulbs and stuff are. I saw them.'

He passed Megan a torch. That's odd, she thought. He's very well prepared.

They crept down to the kitchen, cautious as thieves. Ash lay like dirty snow in the hearth and moonlight squeezed limply through the edges of the shutters. Torchlight caught the metal tree standing by the fireside, etching in gold the sorrowful face in the trunk, and the cat, the bat and the raven hanging from its branches.

Megan clicked the light switch on and the torch off and went to sort out the tools they'd need. It wasn't difficult: on a shelf near the door lay a neat row made up of a claw hammer, chisel and wrench. Next to them, tidily folded, was a small hessian bag. Megan frowned. 'I've got what we want. It's funny though.'

'What is?' Brand's eyes widened with pretend innocence.

'Those tools and the bag — all laid out, waiting for us to find them. I don't suppose you know anything about that?'

Brand wasn't very good at lying.

'It was Alyson, wasn't it,' Megan insisted. 'She put these

101

out ready. You told her we know where the violin's hidden. Oh, Brand, you promised!'

He wheedled horribly: 'I couldn't help it. It just ... sort of came out.'

'I suppose Alyson told you all that stuff about Dad and Brian Walmsley not letting us join in a search, or giving us credit for working out where the Guarneri's hidden? And I bet she suggested you didn't tell Dad and looked for it yourself.'

Brand nodded dumbly, then burst out, 'Anyway, it's true. They won't let us, will they?'

'Probably not,' she admitted.

'So can we go and look? Please.'

It was hard to refuse him, especially when she felt the same. What made her uneasy was wondering why Alyson wanted them to find the violin rather than Brian Walmsley. Maybe she hoped it would make him look foolish if two children succeeded where he'd failed.

'All right, we'll do it.'

'Yes!' Brand whooped.

'But only if we tell Dad straight after.'

'OK,' he said cheerfully.

A shadow rose up from the chair by the hearth, with a faint brushing noise like unfolding velvet.

'Hello, Pywackett,' Brand said.

Long, yellow eyes regarded him unblinkingly.

'I thought Alyson took her home after work,' Megan said.

The cat followed them to the door and tried to push her way out. Megan's foot stopped her. A growl boiled in the cat's throat. Megan managed to pull her foot away and close the door without hurting the cat. She left it snarling on the other side.

Megan and Brand followed the sliding torch beam down the corridor and up to the painted door. It hovered over the violin. Tiny brush strokes stood out in little furrows, spoiling the illusion of reality.

Brand slipped his hand into Megan's and they hurried across the monochrome hall, up the moon-silvered stairs and into the cavernous emptiness of the east wing. The bloom of yellow torchlight rode the tunnelled darkness to the junk-room door.

Inside furniture loomed, lurching monsters trapped together in unfamiliar darkness.

Megan balanced the torch on a chair and angled its beam in the direction of the hidden door.

'Let's shift that chest of drawers.'

It only took a moment and didn't make too much noise, only a sickly scraping on the floorboards like fingernails down an old-fashioned blackboard.

Megan stretched out her hand to pick up the torch. It rolled away down the plush seat and lit the mirror from below. She reached for it. Her mirror-image did the same. Behind the reflected Megan, stood a shrouded figure watching the real Megan.

She fiercely clamped down a yelp of terror so as not to frighten Brand and screwed her eyes shut.

There couldn't be anyone behind her. There was nothing in the room except for old furniture wrapped in shadow. Her hand groped for the torch, found it, turned it away from the mirror. She looked up. Without illumination the mirror was a dead eye, blank, empty.

'Time to go.' Megan coughed away the husky scratch of fear in her voice.

She led the way into the stairwell where the darkness was shades blacker and the coldness degrees more bitter than before. The torch beam fingered the stairs, pointed at the door in the wall.

'Come on.' Megan tugged at her brother's arm.

'What if it isn't there?'

'What if it is? Just imagine, you'll be the first person to see it in a hundred and fifty years.'

Brand's face, eerily lit upside down from the torch, lifted towards Megan's. 'D'you really think so?'

'Let's go and find out' Megan opened the door and they went through on to the balcony.

On the dome, silver stars glittered untarnished in the kindly light of the moon. Under them the nine muses danced.

Megan dropped her bag at the foot of Euterpe's panel. This plan was stupid. She felt faintly sick as though she were walking on a flimsy plank across a bottomless chasm. But it was too late to give up now. She'd promised Brand. She couldn't let him down, break his heart all over again. 'We'll have to be careful. We don't want to wreck it.'

She passed the torch to Brand and ran her hands down the side of the panel. 'There's strips of wood holding it in place. If we get one side off we might be able to slide the panel out.' She picked up the chisel. 'Here we go.'

She prised the tool under the strip of beading and levered upwards. Wood cracked and a piece fell away. Then another. Then two more. At last the whole side was clear.

'It's fitted in quite tightly.' Megan said. 'I think it might be glued.' She worked the claw hammer into the top and pushed, slowly.

A horrible rending echoed round the gallery.

A gap opened up. Megan tugged.

'Grab the bottom,' she ordered. Brand pushed his fingers into the gap and pulled at the panel. Old glue snapped, cracking like pistol shots. The muse leaped forward into Megan's arms. A cloud of ancient dust billowed out of the hollow Euterpe had been shielding. 'Gross!' Brand coughed, backing away and furiously wafting at the grey dirt. Megan balanced Euterpe against one of her sisters. Brand passed over the torch. 'Fingers crossed,' Megan said.

She shone the torch into the empty space. Dust swirled

in the beam. Behind a cloud of whirling particles a dark shape leaned into the back wall. Brand reached in and grasped it. He drew the shape out and held it up for Megan to see. It was a violin case.

Megan felt a huge grin spread over her face, exactly like the one she saw on Brand's as he held the case gently, almost reverently.

She slid the painted panel back into place. The pieces of beading only took moments to press down the sides again, the nails slotting loosely into position.

Suddenly dark flecks flickered over the panel, speckling it with moving smuts. Bats! Bats darting over the dome, casting their brief shadows on to Euterpe. They're inspecting us, Megan thought. There was always something watching in The House: monkeys, peacocks, even the friendly owl on his newel post.

The bats went, as abruptly as they'd arrived.

Megan and Brand went straight to Brand's room and placed the case on a table. Brand brushed dust off the black leather case then wiped his hands down his jeans. Megan watched him push up the gold clasp, lift the lid. And there, cradled in scarlet velvet, lay the Guarneri Del Gesù violin.

The Guarneri Del Gesù

Megan marvelled at her little brother's confidence as he picked up the violin. She'd never dare turn it over and over as he did, nor move her hands over it so casually. 'It's broken,' she said.

Brand shook his head. 'The bridge's collapsed, that's all.' He touched the bridge with a careful finger and it moved. He tilted the instrument slightly and something rattled downwards. 'That's the soundpost gone. And the strings.' Two strings curled upwards and two down.

Megan reached into the case and picked up the bow, a long slender wand of glossy black wood. The ivory handle felt smooth as she wafted the bow to and fro. Tails and threads of brittle horsehair drifted outwards. 'I suppose this needs doing up too.'

Brand didn't seem to hear. He was busy looking through the violin's sound holes.

'What are you doing?' Megan asked.

'Seeing what the label says.' He tilted it into the light. 'I.H.S., some writing, 1732 and a cross with leaves on it.'

'Like the one on the door!'

Brand was too happy to say, I told you so.

In her mind's eye Megan compared the violin in Brand's hands with the painting. It was a darker colour, less glossy. And with the fallen bridge it seemed quite different. 'Are you sure it really is the Guarneri?'

'Yes.' His child's voice was full of the authority that came with knowledge. He pointed: 'It's got the same long, thin sound holes, and the same silver stars in the pegs. And look at the pattern on the wood — it's the same as well, squashed up in the middle and wide at the edges.'

Megan's mental comparison didn't include any of those details. It showed how important the violin was to Brand that he'd noticed so much. She slotted the bow back into place enjoying the feel of plush velvet under her fingers.

'Now we have to tell Dad,' she said. 'You can look after the Guarneri while I fetch him. I wonder how he's going to take it!'

Brand cradled the violin protectively, as though it were a baby.

Dad didn't want to wake up. Eventually he grasped that Megan wanted him to go to Brand. Then he came to, alarmed.

'It's all right,' Megan reassured him. 'Brand's just got something really important to tell you.'

Dad grumbled his way into his dressing-gown and stumbled to Brand's room like a bear only just out of hibernation.

Brand stood beside his little table, the Guarneri now back in its case. 'We found it, Dad,' he said.

'So I see.' Dad moved like an automaton over to the table. 'You haven't touched it!' he said, aghast.

'Oh yes.' Brand took the violin out and gave it to Dad. It looked absurdly fragile in his enormous hands.

'I'm not sure we should be doing this,' Dad said. 'Put it in the case, Brand.' He passed it hastily back.

'I need to sit down.' Dad collapsed on to the bed. Megan and Brand perched one on either side of him. 'Now, tell me, where was the violin and how did you find it?'

They took it in turns to explain, the story tumbling out in sections. Neither of them mentioned Alyson's part in the search. Dad winced when Megan described prising away the painted panel of Euterpe. She hurried on and let Brand finish the tale.

When it was over Dad sat in silence, his head in his

hands. Megan and Brand exchanged worried glances over his bowed head.

Dad dropped his hands at last. 'Let me get this straight. I told you quite clearly not to go searching without permission. You not only disobeyed that instruction you deliberately withheld information; you risked breaking your necks clambering up staircases and on potentially lethal walkways in the dark; you almost certainly damaged a rare and valuable Pre-Raphaelite tempera panel and you stole a priceless eighteenth-century violin.'

Megan's heart sank. She didn't dare look at Brand; she knew his eyes would be filling with tears. Dad was cruel. It wasn't Brand's fault, it was hers; she was the one who'd made the final decision not to tell Dad.

Dad gave a roar of laughter and threw his arms around them. Megan felt herself squashed nose to nose with Brand against Dad's chest with his laughter rumbling against her cheek. She realised with a shock that it was his first real, deep-down laugh since Mum had died.

Dad released them enough so that they could breathe. 'I've got two bloody marvellous children. Bright,' he kissed the top of Megan's head, 'brave,' he kissed Brand. 'And talk about showing initiative!' The rumble in his chest started again. The laugh filled the room. Brand joined in. Then Megan. They laughed until they fell back exhausted.

'Now,' Dad said when he'd got his breath back, 'we have to decide on the next step. I think that's to put the violin in Brian's charge.'

Megan braced herself for a protest from Brand. It didn't come. Maybe he knew in his heart of hearts that he was never going to play the Guarneri.

Dad checked his watch. 'Five thirty! Too early for Brian. I'll ring him later. I wonder how he'll take the news that a couple of children succeeded in doing in a few days what he's failed to do in years?' Dad's grin had a surprising touch of mischief.

He closed the violin case and tucked it securely under his arm. 'Sorry, kids, I have to take charge of this now. I suggest we all try to get a bit of sleep before we take this precious object to Brian.'

This time Megan was sure Brand was going to object. She waited for him to plead with Dad to leave the Guarneri with him at least until they saw Brian Walmsley. Instead he waited for Dad to leave then dragged the duvet over himself and pretended to look sleepy.

Megan couldn't think what he was up to. She was too tired to care much. 'Goodnight — or, good-morning,' she said.

Brand grunted. He was definitely play-acting. At least he was shamming on purpose. It wasn't the same as him behaving as though Mum were still alive.

Megan went along with the pretence and tiptoed out, gently pushing the connecting door closed. Just before it clicked into place she heard Brand's bed creak as if he were sitting up. She waited, holding the door very slightly open. There was a crackling, papery sort of noise then the sound of Brand humming softly. He carried on, first in little bursts, then in longer phrases.

Megan shut the door quietly so as not to disturb him. This was more like the old Brand, a small boy happily doing his music thing. If Dad knew he'd say, as he did so often, It's a good sign. This time Megan would agree with him.

The Ivy Crown

Morning light slotted itself along Hob's Lane. In the doorway of Magna Strings, Brian Walmsley was waiting as Dad had arranged. The elastic smile wasn't in evidence. His eyes, which didn't smile either, went straight to the sheet-wrapped bundle in Dad's arms. He turned and rang the doorbell.

A very tall, thin man, much younger than Megan had imagined, opened it wide. 'Brian, and friends. I've been expecting you.' His eyes, like Brian Walmsley's, fixed on Dad's bundle. An eyebrow raised itself like a question mark. 'Please, come in,' he said dryly.

He led them through a modest front sales room into a quiet annexe where cellos, held upright by their scrolls, stood in racks around the walls; violas hung in ranks; bows lined up on boards in neat rows. And everywhere — in racks, on stands — were violins, polished and glossy, in every shade from pale gold to conker-brown.

Megan and Brand followed the others into a small, cluttered workshop. A sharp smell of rosin, varnish and glue filled Megan's nostrils.

The violin dealer sat behind a bench, arms folded, subtle as an enchanter with his magic nostrums all around — pots, tins, glasses — glistening with arcane substances.

He extended his hand to Dad. 'Daniel Turner,' he said by way of introduction.

'Michael Foster,' Dad answered, 'and these are my children, Megan and Brand.'

The violin dealer solemnly shook hands with them too. 'I'm very pleased to meet you.'

He sounded as if he meant it.

Dad unwrapped the violin case on the workbench.

'Very nice,' Daniel said. 'Victorian. French walnut. Custom made.'

Dad clicked the catches open while Daniel took off his watch and laid it by the exploded carcass of a chocolate-brown cello. He put on a white apron, flexed his fingers and picked up the violin. Right hand round the neck, left supporting the base, he held it at arm's length.

'Good shape.'

He rested it on his knee and regarded it for a long moment

His hands spun it round.

Megan was glad she'd already seen Brand treat the violin in the same way. It meant she didn't wince like Brian Walmsley did when the sound post rattled loudly.

'Minor cracks. Slight split in the seams.' His thumb slid rapidly all round the edges. 'A miracle it's not falling apart.'

He squinted through the sinuous sound holes and a most peculiar smile tweaked his mouth into a kind of restrained gloating. '*Joseph Guarnerius fecit Cremone anno 1732, I.H.S.*,' he read out. 'Let's hope we've got an original label in there.'

The violin went back into its case. Daniel Turner hung up his apron. 'Well,' he said strapping on his watch. 'The Devonport Guarneri Del Gesù has surfaced again at last. Where's it been hiding all these generations?'

'Megan found it,' Brand said proudly. 'She worked it out.'

Daniel's expressive eyebrow raised itself again.

'Tell us, Megan,' Dad said. 'Even Brian doesn't know the whole story. I only told him a bit of it over the phone. I thought he'd want to know it all from the true discoverer.'

Megan wasn't so sure. She told the story straight to Daniel, trying not to sneak a look at Brian Walmsley to see how he was taking it.

Daniel's reaction was very satisfying. 'Ingenious,' he said. 'You have a sharp mind. Brian's never mentioned Lettice's poems as far as I remember.'

Brian Walmsley went on the defensive. 'I don't like poetry much. I never got round to reading Lettice's book properly.'

Daniel's eyebrow quirked sceptically. 'We'll take the violin to London for authentication and restoration. I'll ring now.'

'Now!' Megan said, startled, as Daniel headed for his little office.

'Of course,' he said over his shoulder.

Brian Walmsley tidied the sheet round the violin case.

'Legally I'm in charge of this until Head Office gives me instructions so I'll go with Daniel.'

He's putting himself back in control, Megan thought.

Daniel came back. 'We're expected in a few hours,' he told Brian Walmsley.

They've had this set up for ages, Megan realised, just in case. Now it's happened and it's all out of our hands.

'It's not right!' she blurted out. Four pairs of eyes looked at her with surprise. 'Well, it's not,' she went on defiantly. 'We found the violin and you're taking it away. We'll probably never see it again and Brand will never get to play it.'

'You play?' Daniel asked Brand.

'Yes.'

Daniel picked up a violin and a bow from his worktop. 'Then play.'

Shocked, Megan glanced at Dad. His face was closed, tight.

Brand tucked the instrument under his chin, nestling it warmly into his neck. Unhesitatingly he drew the bow across the strings. One shivering note thrilled through the room. Brand adjusted the pegs, played again. Eventually he was satisfied with the tuning. He played. Only scales

112

and arpeggios, then a simple, slow, imperfectly remembered piece.

He didn't play well, even Megan knew that. She didn't care. It was sweet music because he made it. His fingers fumbled. He recovered, played on.

Megan hoped her quiet tears would pass unnoticed. But a handkerchief pushed into her fist. She wiped her eyes, grateful for the crisp, fresh-smelling cotton. She offered the handkerchief back.

'Keep it,' Brian Walmsley said softly.

'Stop,' Daniel ordered Brand. 'You haven't practised in a long time.'

Megan opened her mouth to protest at his callousness. Brian Walmsley shook his head warningly.

'Take the violin and practise properly,' Daniel said.

'Mum says I don't practise enough.'

'Then she's a wise woman,' Daniel said. 'Is she a musician too?'

Dad spoke before Brand could answer. 'My wife was a fine violinist and teacher. She thought that one day Brand might play well too.'

A look of understanding passed between Dad and Daniel Turner. The violin-maker inclined his head briefly for a moment in a gesture of regret. Then he picked up a battered old case and gave it to Brand. He put the violin and bow away and tucked the case under his arm.

Brian Walmsley was impatient to be off. He went into Hob's Lane with Dad while Daniel and Brand pottered about collecting rosin and spare strings. Megan couldn't help feeling a small surge of pleasure at Brian Walmsley's resentment and another at her own triumph.

At last they were all ready and set off down Hob's Lane, Brian Walmsley hurrying ahead with Dad and Brand. Brand carried the violin case confidently, as though the months of lost music had never been.

Megan clutched at the handkerchief. It had gone cold

and clammy. She thrust it to the bottom of her pocket.

'Don't take any notice of Brian,' Daniel said. 'He's too stunned to be properly grateful. Give him time.'

Megan ignored the kindly advice. 'I bet he's jealous. He's been searching for years and I worked it out in a few days.'

'Jealous? No. Well, perhaps a little. What you've got to understand is that for Brian — and me — finding the Guarneri is equivalent to discovering Tutankhamun's tomb.'

Megan couldn't see why Daniel wanted to make allowances for Brian Walmsley's creepy manner. He was so ... greasy. Maybe that wasn't a good enough reason for disliking him quite so much. He'd never actually done anything to earn it, apart from frightening her a few times when he'd really been trying to help.

They stepped out of the shelter of Hob's Lane. Wind snarled and thrashed at shoppers in the open square and hurled litter at passers-by. A drumbeat summoned shoppers to the war memorial.

'The morris men are back,' Brand grinned.

The men stamped, jingling ankle bells and flourishing their red handkerchiefs in the grasping air. The fiddler struck up a tune.

'The music,' Brand said. 'It's the music!'

'What's he talking about?' Megan said, bewildered.

Dad was no help. 'Don't ask me.'

'We need to go,' Brian Walmsley said.

'Wait a bit,' Dad said. 'I want to get a few things sorted with you.'

Brian Walmsley impatiently poked a wrist out of a sleeve and checked his watch. 'We have to get going.'

'I'll walk to the car with you then. Megan, keep an eye on Brand for a minute or two till I get back.'

'All right.' This time she didn't mind staying with Brand: she wanted to find out why he was excited about the music. She listened to it carefully. It did sound a bit familiar.

A circlet of leaves tossed to and fro between the dancers. That was it — it was the dance the men had done before, the one the two girls had giggled and wolf-whistled at.

There was more to it though. Megan thought the tune seemed a bit like the one Brand had hummed last night when she'd listened covertly through the connecting door. But surely that had been slower and more sad?

The dancers circled, scarlet leg ribbons writhing, handkerchiefs whirling.

A rasping 'caw' sounded above Megan. She turned her face up and the wind spread her hair round it like a net. A raven perched on one arm of the cross, his ragged wings sticking out for balance, his claws scrabbling for purchase on the polished granite.

The drum beat on. The fiddler's fingers scampered up and down like skinny mice.

A soft blow fell on Megan's head. 'Support the Men of Stretton.' The Fool hit her again with his red balloon. He held out his cap expectantly and jingled it. Megan felt in her pocket. The Fool's orange and yellow rags licked round him like flames in the fretting wind.

Megan dropped silver in his cap. 'What's this dance called?' she asked.

'The Ivy Crown,' said the Fool. 'It's based on a local courtship dance. Around the end of autumn lads wove crowns out of ivy — to symbolise perpetual love — and danced with them. At the end they presented their chosen girl with the crown. She put it on to show she accepted him and they were married in the spring.'

'What if she refused?'

'You wouldn't want to know.'

With a final terrific yell, the music stopped and the dance ended. The leader broke free of the ring of men. Holding the ivy crown he came towards Megan. The drum

115

rolled softly. The dancer stopped in front of Megan. He offered her the crown.

'No thank you.'

The drum beat louder, faster. The man pressed forward.

'I don't want it!' Megan insisted.

The red balloon batted at her head. 'Take it,' the Fool said. 'Bad luck otherwise.'

The dancer lifted the crown.

'I said no!' Megan struck out. The crown flew from the morris man's hand. Wind seized it with a shriek, whirled it high over the market square, hurled it to the ground. The crown bowled over and over, leaves flying like feathers. The drum stopped beating. Hostile faces circled Megan.

'She told you she didn't want it,' Brand said bravely.

An alleyway opened into the tight crowd. Dad came down it, carrying the battered crown. 'Here.' He thrust it at the morris man. 'It was halfway to Hob's Lane when I caught it.'

The dancer contemptuously flung the coronet on to the war memorial steps. Ignoring Megan he nodded at the fiddler. A jaunty tune jigged in time to the singing wind. The dancers fell into a complicated formation chasing an imaginary fox in and out of a maze of interlaced sticks. One by one, led by the Fool, the crowd began to clap in time to the lively music. They forgot about Megan. She walked away with Dad on one side and Brand on the other.

The ivy crown rolled by, snatched from the steps by the wind. It lifted like a Frisbee and landed in a rubbish bin next to a market stall.

A black shape torpedoed overhead and fetched up against the bin. The raven pecked at the crown.

'Clear off!' The stall holder flapped a paper bag. The bird took off.

On the drive back to The House Megan glimpsed the raven every now and then, a black rag tossed about among

116

the mad grey clouds.

The car topped the hill. Below, The House lay like an anchored ship in a thrashing, howling sea of trees.

The raven soared over The House then plunged out of sight behind it.

'There Is a Ghost Here....'

All the way from the ballroom, across the hall and down the corridor, music corruscated through the air, counterpointing the wind's wild song. Brand was playing the violin again.

In the study room Megan began a new section for her assignment: the story of Judith Moone. She worked quickly, writing notes on what she knew so far. When she'd finished, she read them through:

> *A beautiful young woman, Judith Moone, who lived in the seventeenth century, was a witch. She worked at The House in The Hollow, for Sir Walter Devonport, Justice of the Peace. She lived in a cottage in the woods with a pet cat, a raven and a flock of bats. She stole one of Phillip Devonport's gloves (Phillip was Walter's son) and bewitched it. The spell killed him. The steward of The House somehow found this out and told Sir Walter. Sir Walter condemned Judith to death by burning in 1645, on 31 October — Hallowe'en — also known as Samhain.*

Hallowe'en, that was tomorrow! At home Megan and Brand might be going to Hallowe'en parties with their friends. There was no way she'd do that here: The House was sinister enough already.

She looked at her notes again. There weren't that many and there were gaps in Judith's story. Why had she wanted to harm Phillip? How had the steward found out what she'd done? Where exactly had the execution taken place? Megan was sure she remembered the attendant at the museum saying something about Judith haunting the woods where she'd died. Why hadn't she listened more carefully? How could she find out what she wanted to know? There was one way. She'd resisted it up to now but she knew what she had to do. She looked in the back of the library books before she remembered she'd left Brian Walmsley's pamphlet with Dad when she'd told him about the Devonports and the Guarneri. She'd have to ask him what he'd done with it. He probably wouldn't be able to resist teasing her about Brian Walmsley but she almost didn't care: she had to know about Judith.

Megan found Dad in his studio with the door open and half his attention on Brand's playing. 'I can't concentrate,' he grumbled. 'And I can't think what to do next with this story. I need one good, strong image.'

'The man at the museum said Judith the witch stole a glove from Sir Walter's son, Phillip, and bewitched it so he died. They found the glove in her house all wet and stinky and full of thorns.'

Dad's eyes gleamed. He set to work, his pencil flying confidently over the paper.

Megan couldn't interrupt him now, not when he was working well. The pamphlet, and her research, would have to wait.

Megan asked Dad about the pamphlet next morning. He said he'd taken it back to the study and put it on top of the books from Stretton library. Megan couldn't find it on the desk, or under it. She tried the old sofa in the TV room in case Brand had looked at it there in between sessions of watching television. She even pulled the cushions off and looked down the sides. There was no sign of the pamphlet. Just as she'd decided to pester Dad again, Brian Walmsley arrived with news of the Guarneri Del Gesù violin.

He sat at the head of the kitchen table with Megan, Dad and Brand around him like acolytes. Only Alyson carried on with her tasks as though nothing out the ordinary had happened. Even so, Megan was sure she listened carefully to everything Brian Walmsley said.

'Now the violin's with the experts it'll be properly authenticated and then The Trust will decide whether to restore it for exhibition purposes only, or restore it so it can be played again.'

'It's got to be played. It's got to,' Brand said.

He still thought he could play it. Megan wished he'd give up his forlorn hope. 'Which do you want to happen, Mr Walmsley?' she asked.

'Daniel Turner and I discussed it many times, theoretically speaking of course, before we discovered it...'

'We discovered it! Megan bristled with indignation.

Out of the corner of her eye she saw Alyson's mocking face as she glided by with a basketful of ironing. She might have been deriding Brian Walmsley's arrogance, or Megan's anger, or even both.

'...Paganini used to joke,' Brian Walmsley went on, 'that Guarneri only ever built his violins with wood from trees that nightingales sang in. Nightingales shouldn't be kept in cages and violins shouldn't be kept behind glass.'

'You think the Guarneri should be played again then?' Dad asked.

'Oh, yes. And Daniel's opinions count for a lot. He's well respected in the business.'

A sigh of relief gusted from Brand. 'I'm going to practise,' he said. 'Mum says I have to practise if I'm going to be any good. And I am.'

Inevitably Dad asked, 'Go and keep an eye on him, will you Megan?'

She made sure Brand left the ballroom doors open wide then she went into the peacock study and set to work writing up a neat draft of Judith's story so far. She almost forgot Brand; though she was half-aware of his warm-up scales and arpeggios, she ignored them.

He began a slow, sad melody. A cascade of notes pierced its way into Megan's heart like a reproach. She knew that tune from somewhere. She stopped writing and listened. It sounded like the tune Brand had hummed alone in his room after they'd found the Guarneri. It was lovely and she wanted to hear more.

She went softly to the ballroom, careful not to disturb Brand's concentration. He was following some music propped up against a book resting on the music stand Dad had brought down from the junk room.

Megan tiptoed closer, closer — as close as she dared without disturbing Brand's concentration.

Laid on the book of exercise pieces was a single sheet of yellowing old paper. Hand-drawn bars of music slanted across it with an occasional word jotted here and there. Along the bottom flowed two lines of writing in a loose, shapely, hurried-looking script. Megan couldn't read it; it was in a language she didn't understand. She knew what the paper was though.

'Paganini's variation!'

There was a shriek as Brand's bow skidded across the strings. Shock, guilt, defiance all flickered across his face.

'Where did you find it?' Megan demanded.

Brand's knuckles showed white as he clutched the violin. 'In the old violin case.'

'I didn't see it.'

'It was behind the velvet stuff, all folded small, pushed in except a corner poked up. I pulled it out when you went to fetch Dad. I know they won't let me keep it so I took it I was going to copy it out, honest, then give it to Mr Walmsley.'

'Come and do it now. If you're quick you can make a copy before they've finished talking.'

Megan's persuasion worked. Brand soon scrawled down a reasonable copy for himself.

Megan picked up the original. She tried to read the two lines at the bottom: *Devo lasciare questa casa. Qui c'è un fantasma e quella ragazza è pazza!* It had to be Italian because Paganini had written it. Must be a musical instruction, Megan decided.

'Do you think Dad and Mr Walmsley'll be mad at me?' Brand asked.

'I bet they'll be too excited at finding an original manuscript in Paganini's own handwriting to care.'

They were. Brian Walmsley handled the sheet of paper as though it were incredibly precious. He placed it reverently on the table. Words struggled out: 'The lost variation. Paganini didn't burn it after all.'

'It must've been in the fire at some stage,' Dad said. 'The edges are charred.'

'Perhaps it fell out of the fire-grate and one of the servants found it and gave it to Lettice.'

Megan thought it was more likely Lettice herself had gone into Paganini's room after he'd left, searching for some trace of her hero to keep. The manuscript would have been better than anything she could have dreamed up herself.

'I don't suppose we'll ever know now.' Brian Walmsley shrugged. 'It doesn't matter.'

He read out the inscription on the bottom. His accent sounded convincing, very musical and fluent Megan knew he understood what the writing meant.

'What does it say?'

'I must get out of this house. There's a ghost here and the girl is mad!'

Dad barked out a laugh. 'We all know who the mad girl was ...'

'Lettuce,' Brand said.

'Lett-eece,' Megan and Brian Walmsley corrected together.

'...but who,' Dad went on, 'was the ghost?'

'Play for us, Brand.' They'd all forgotten about Alyson. 'Play it,' she repeated. 'No one ever expected to hear it. It was lost for ever. I'll be interested to hear what it sounds like.'

'We all will,' snapped Brian Walmsley.

Brand chewed his lip uncertainly.

'I'd like to hear it...' Megan only just managed to stop herself adding, 'again'.

'Go on, son,' Dad said. 'I'm curious too.'

'Told you they wouldn't be mad,' Megan whispered, and winked.

Brand squeezed his eyes in response, which was the nearest he could get to a wink. 'I've been practising,' he said, tucking the instrument under his chin and flexing his bowing arm. 'It's a variation on The Ivy Crown, you know, that dance the morris men were doing, with the wreath thing.'

That was where Megan had heard it before! But Paganini had mixed it all up for his variation and made it slower and more melancholy. It was no wonder she hadn't recognised it.

The music flowed and the tune tugged at Megan's memory again, and not only because she'd heard Brand humming it two nights ago. There was still more to it.

Dad and Brian Walmsley listened intently. Alyson had her eyes closed and swayed slightly to the tempo as she'd done when she listened to the fiddler in the square.

The pace quickened a little. The melody felt more and more familiar. Megan concentrated furiously.

Crash!

The noise came from the studio.

Dad got there first, the others close behind. The studio was a shambles, drawings scattered everywhere, ink splashed over the table, the chair overturned.

Paganini regarded Megan enigmatically from the floor where his portrait lay among the scatter of Dad's drawings.

From behind her Megan heard Alyson say, 'There is a ghost here...'

***

Tight-lipped, furious, Dad wouldn't let anyone help clear up the mess. The studio was his territory. Alyson and Brian Walmsley went to the kitchen. Megan took Brand to the TV room and they played card games fast, one after the other. They didn't mention what had happened. After the third game, Brand complained that he was bored.

'I'll go and see what's happening in the kitchen,' Megan said.

Brand caught at her sleeve. 'Don't be long.'

As Megan approached the kitchen, she heard Brian Walmsley's angry voice. 'You've got to stop it now, Alyson.'

Megan paused.

'Not after three hundred and fifty years of waiting; not when I'm this close.'

'It's not safe. Look at what's just happened! It didn't matter at first. He was only shifting things around, messing up papers. Now he's created havoc with Michael's work. You don't know how strong he's capable of getting when he's really frightened.'

They knew who'd wrecked the studio! Why hadn't they told Dad?

Megan sidled closer to the doorway.

'You're such a coward, Brian.' Alyson's voice was contemptuous and amused.

'And you're reckless, stupidly reckless.'

'Not reckless, daring maybe. I take my chances where I can and this is the best one since Paganini. All the other scraping fiddlers we got into The House were only local men too scared to do as they were told. Paganini should've been different, at ease with the supernatural. In the end he was no better.'

'Stop now or I'll stop you.'

'I don't think so,' Alyson taunted.

A soft, heavy lump banged into Megan's legs. Pywackett

124

barged past into the kitchen mewling as if she were about to be sick.

Megan followed her in. 'I wondered if you wanted any help.'

'No thank you,' Alyson said. She stroked Pywackett and settled her into the chair by the hearth.

She knows I was listening, Megan worried. She must do.

Brian Walmsley knew too. 'I'm going,' he said to Megan. 'A word of warning first. Be careful, Alyson wants something from you.'

The housekeeper smiled pityingly at Brian Walmsley. 'Take no notice, Megan.'

Megan didn't want to get involved in their quarrel. She ignored both of them.

Brian Walmsley left.

'You don't like each other much, you and Mr Walmsley,' she said.

'I despise him and he distrusts me. It's because I know things he finds hard to accept and prefers to ignore — when he can. Rather like your father, which is why I can't tell him yet who's intent on spoiling his work. At the moment it's easier for him to blame me than acknowledge the truth.'

'Do you really know who it is?'

Alyson nodded, a smile fluttering round her mouth like a moth round a dangerous flame.

'Who was it then?'

'Read Brian's pamphlet and when you do, don't make the mistake of thinking he's a fool.'

Megan went back to the TV room but Brand was playing in the ballroom again, so she turned to the studio. Dad sat staring at the ruined drawings piled up on the table. From the top the revenant glared balefully.

'They don't seem too bad,' Megan consoled.

'They're not really, except for this latest series. I was

pleased with that glove story you told me, Megan. It was a good one. Gave me all sorts of ideas. Look.'

He smoothed out a ripped, ink-stained storyboard showing Judith's accuser, Jacob, stealing a glove from a chest of drawers in a grand bedroom then piercing it through and through with thorns. The last couple of pictures showed him planting it under some bricks round the hearth in the witch's cottage.

'In fact,' Dad said, 'I like the idea so much, I'm going to draw this up again.'

Megan only half listened. Her eyes darted from the pictures of Jacob to the one of the revenant and back again.

Alyson's voice chimed in Megan's ear as clearly as if they'd been standing side by side: Read Brian's pamphlet and don't make the mistake of thinking he's a fool.

Megan *had* thought Brian Walmsley a fool, because he'd been too arrogant to read Lettice's poems. Now she knew she was a fool too, and for the same sort of reason.

The Revenant

Megan knew the pamphlet had to be in the study some-where. She searched under the tables and behind the curtains. If only she hadn't let her dislike of Brian Walmsley put her off reading it before now. He thought Lettice was no more than a silly, over-excitable girl who couldn't possibly write anything worth reading. Because of his prejudice he'd missed the poem with the clues about the violin. She'd dismissed his pamphlet in the same way. Not any more though. She tugged an old armchair away from the wall. There it was! She snatched up the crum-pled pamphlet, pushed the chair back and curled up in it. She smoothed the pamphlet out and began to read.

The House in Hopkins's Hollow has its own ghost: Jacob Fisher, Steward of The House from 1640 to 1683. In the autumn of 1645 he approached his employer, local mag-istrate Sir Walter Devonport. Jacob denounced a young woman, Judith Moone, as a witch, saying she had cursed Sir Walter's son, Phillip, and caused his death. Why Jacob did so is a mystery but legend says he asked Judith to partner him in a dance and she refused. This angered him to such a degree that he invented a story about her bewitching Phillip's glove, drenching it in cat urine, pierc-ing it with thorns and burying it to rot away in the ground. As the glove decayed, so Phillip wasted away until he died. Jacob also accused Judith of using 'familiars', animal spies: Pywackett, a cat, Hodge, a raven, and The Knotted Cloude, a flock of bats.

Sir Walter condemned her to death by burning and she was executed on 31 October 1645 at a site in Stretton Woods.

Jacob Fisher lost his wits, some say because Judith cursed him as she died. Whatever the reason, Jacob fled to The House after the execution and died there in 1683. There have been many reported sightings of his ghost.

Megan lowered the pamphlet.

That was it then: it was Jacob Fisher's ghost, Dad's revenant, who was causing all the trouble, doing all the damage. But why was he reacting so violently? How could it actually harm him if people found out he'd set Judith up and accused her falsely because he was angry she'd rejected his ivy crown? It didn't make sense. But then, Megan knew what it was like to be so ashamed of something that you'd do anything to keep it a secret.

The strains of Paganini's *Variation on The Ivy Crown* echoed from the ballroom. I bet Jacob doesn't like that, Megan thought uneasily. Brian Walmsley's anxiety about what Jacob might do next came back to her. She'd better make sure Dad knew what was going on.

For once Megan went into the studio without knocking. 'I know who trashed your pictures,' Megan blurted out before Dad had a chance to protest. 'Jacob's been trying to stop you telling Judith's story.'

'Jacob who?'

'Draw, Dad, and I'll tell you.' Megan thrust his pencil at him.

He hesitated.

'At least this way you'll end up with a proper plot.'

Dad grunted sceptically. He took the pencil anyway.

Megan pulled up the stool. She put the finished drawings in order. 'Start your story with the dance picture. This is Judith, the witch. Only she isn't. She's just a young, pretty woman and Jacob fancies her like mad. He weaves her an ivy crown.'

Brand's music flowed lightly along the corridor and filled the studio with background music.

Dad's fingers flew over the paper, drawing the revenant with a young man's face. He was holding out a coronet of leaves. 'Now why did I draw him?' Dad said, bemused.

'It's that ambience you're always talking about. The House has got a story and you really are tuned into it. The revenant is Jacob. He gives the ivy crown to Judith as a token that he wants to marry her. She refuses it.'

Dad showed Jacob's shock, his hurt and then his fury.

Megan added the crumpled drawings of Jacob stealing the glove and planting it in Judith's cottage. 'Jacob accuses Judith to Sir Walter Devonport,' she said.

The pencil conjured up a moonless night, Jacob huddled in the shadows, Sir Walter, grim, powerful, by his side.

Megan placed the drawing of Judith in prison next to the hurried sketches. 'He interrogates Judith.'

The hasty sequence of sketches showed a candlelit figure, advancing towards Judith crouched in the corner of a dark cell; Judith's mouth pleading; Judith's hands warding off the Justice.

Brand's music slowed, dropped into a minor key.

'Sir Walter condemns Judith.' Megan put the polished drawing of the court scene in place. The scarlet of Judith's gown blossomed across the page, 'Sir Walter sentences her to death. She's taken to the woods to be burned.'

Another series of drawings flowed rapidly from under Dad's hand: Judith dragged to the pyre; pinioned to the stake; flames rising; merciful smoke choking upwards.

The music quickened, fast as flames tearing through kindling.

'Judith curses Jacob.'

A blast of cold malignant air billowed through the studio. A tall, gaunt figure loomed over Megan and Dad: the figure whom Megan had seen reflected in the kitchen window and the junk-room mirror; the figure who had visited her at night and spied on her in the study; the figure who had appeared in her dreams and Brand's and

Paganini's; the revenant in Dad's drawings.

Jacob reached down, seized Dad's wrist and shook it. The pencil flew across the room.

The music changed tempo, flew lightly, happily, like skipping feet.

Jacob hurled himself at Dad's storyboard. Pictures flew, pencils careened across the table, ink splashed on the floor.

'What —!' Dad never finished. Jacob slammed into him, clawing, punching. Dad was plucked from the chair, skidded across the floor and crashed into the wall. Jacob tossed the chair across the room. It twirled crazily round and round.

'Stop!' Alyson's voice, calm and firm, carried through the studio.

The chair stopped spinning. Pens and pencils completed their roll down the table and fetched up in the trough. In the stillness Dad's laboured breathing was the only sound. Brand stared, white-faced, from behind Alyson's back.

'Go, Jacob,' Alyson ordered the steward. 'I'll call you back when you're required.'

Jacob resisted. His arms waved slowly like waterweed in an undertow. He grew insubstantial. Dissolved to nothing.

Dad sat up. 'Will someone please tell me what's going on,' he wheezed.

Brand ran to Dad and tried to tug him upright. 'Are you all right?' he asked, his face pinched with fear.

Dad pretended to lean for support on Brand. It made Brand look smaller and more fragile than ever. Megan was glad of Dad's pretence. It saved her from going to help him. She didn't think she could.

'I'm pretty sure I'm OK,' — Dad brushed off dust and plaster — 'except for my dignity and sanity. I suppose I have to believe that was a poltergeist.'

'It was Jacob,' Megan told him.

'Who?' Brand asked from under Dad's arm.

'Jacob Fisher, Dad's revenant. Didn't you see him?'

'No.'

'Neither did I,' Dad said. 'Are you sure you weren't seeing things, Megan?'

'Of course not! You heard Alyson tell him to go, didn't you? She saw him too.'

Alyson nodded. 'It was Jacob Fisher. He didn't like you drawing Judith's true story.'

'What story?' Brand said.

'He was once the steward here and it was because of him that Judith was burned as a witch,' Megan said.

'I can tell the full story, if you want to know it.' Alyson held out a pencil to Dad and gestured to the chair she'd wheeled back into place at the drawing table.

Dad took the pencil and sat down just as he had for Megan. 'It would be nice to know why I got chucked across the room, I suppose.' He turned reluctantly back to the drawing board. 'Right, off we go again.'

'Judith didn't curse Jacob,' Alyson said. 'It was her sister, who really was a witch, though no one knew until that moment.'

Dad began to draw. Megan stared in horrified fascination as Dad's sketch took shape, wondering what mischief had made him draw Alyson as Judith's sister. She stole a glance at the housekeeper. Her face stayed impassive.

Megan turned to the drawing again. It showed the witch-Alyson, pointing at Jacob, her beautiful face terrible in the firelight. Then Jacob shrinking away.

'Jacob returned to The House. He never left it again and died there. He was buried in an unmarked pauper's grave. Nobody knew where, except for Judith's sister and nobody cared.' Alyson's voice dripped sweet satisfaction like honey. It made Megan feel sick.

If Dad felt the same way it didn't show: he drew steadily on making Jacob into a cloth-wrapped bundle taken out at night, tossed into a lime-pit outside the town. To one side of the yawning pit he drew a huge black cat, to the other a stalking raven, while overhead a swirl of lines formed a cloud of bats blotting out the light of moon and stars.

Alyson placed the title page at the end of the row of drawings. Jacob, malign and fearful, challenged the faces around him.

'And that's it?' Dad said. 'The end of the story?'

'So far, but it needn't finish there. Because Judith was wrongly executed as a witch her spirit can never find rest. She's trapped in the woods where she died. She can't be freed unless Jacob goes to her, admits his lies and begs her forgiveness. That was the binding hex Judith's sister laid on him. If it's broken then Judith's soul can be set free and that would be the true and rightful end to the story.'

'And just how is Jacob supposed to be persuaded out of the safety of The House and into the woods? He hasn't seemed too eager to leave so far.'

'Well now, that's another strand to the story.'

'Tell us,' Megan said.

'Let's go and sit round the table. It'll be more comfortable than standing about here.'

Dad collected up his pictures.

'They're quite safe,' Alyson sounded amused. 'Jacob won't appear again until I summon him. He's frightened of me.'

'I'm sure he is,' Dad said. 'I'm still not prepared to take any chances. I'm tired of redoing my drawings.'

Alyson was last out of the studio. Megan turned and watched her close the door. She was smiling triumphantly to herself.

Breaking the Hex

'Why didn't you tell us this tale from the beginning?' Dad demanded.

'You wouldn't have believed me,' Alyson said and Megan knew she was right.

'It would've been nice if you'd tried,' Dad said, hugging his bruised ribs. 'It might have spared me some pain.'

Alyson was unmoved. 'You weren't very open to suggestion if you remember.'

Dad just grunted.

Megan interrupted impatiently, 'What about Judith?'

'For the first time in three and a half centuries circumstances are right for us to free her,' Alyson's eyes lit on Brand. 'If you're willing to help.'

Brand wriggled fingers stiff with too much practice.

'On the 31 October, 1646,' Alyson continued, 'a year after Judith's death, the people of Stretton Magna went to the woods to re-enact her burning. They did this year after year. Over time they forgot exactly why they came to the woods and the anniversary became nothing more than an excuse to build a bonfire and clear a ring for dancing. Eventually it merged in their minds with Guy Fawkes' night and took place on 5 November instead of 31 October. Even now, when the true historical facts are on display at the museum, the townspeople insist on lighting the fire on Guy Fawkes night instead of Samhain.'

'Hallowe'en,' Megan remembered.

'And the ancient festival of the dead. On Samhain, ways between the worlds of the living and the unliving open up and souls slip in and out between the two. It's a time when Judith comes to the dancing ring where she died and waits for Jacob Fisher to fulfil the terms of the hex.'

The dancing ring was Judith's execution site! The place where Megan had innocently watched the mock funeral pyre growing, watched Robin add fuel to the waiting fire.

'Fear stopped Jacob leaving The House in life,' Alyson said, 'and it stops him leaving it now. There's only one way to get him out and into the woods.'

'And what's that?' Dad asked suspiciously.

'Tomorrow night is Samhain. Someone must play *The Ivy Crown*. The curse will force Jacob to dance to his tune. Jacob will follow step by step to the execution site. The fiddler will keep playing and draw Jacob on until he's circled the lighted fire three times. When the dance ends Judith will appear, Jacob will confess to his crime and ask her forgiveness. She will grant it and be free. And so, after a fashion, will Jacob.'

'How odd you know exactly what to do,' Dad said. He held up his drawing of the woman cursing Jacob. Kitchen firelight flicked redly over the planes of her beautiful face.

Alyson laughed. 'I don't think I look quite three hundred and fifty years old.'

'It is you,' Megan protested.

'It isn't, you silly child, though we do have the same name. I told you, it's Judith's sister, who really was a witch, a hedge witch, a healer. After she cursed Jacob she fled for her life and only returned years later when the worst of the witch persecutions were over. She brought a respectable husband with her and a daughter, also named Alyson. She trained her and passed the story of Judith and Jacob on to her and she, in turn, passed it to her daughter, Alyson, and so on down the generations to me, I am the last of that female line.'

'I can play *The Ivy Crown*.' Brand's bald statement made Megan's heart jump.

'I don't think so,' Dad said.

'I want to.'

134

Dad hesitated. Megan knew he was torn: he wanted to give Brand what he asked for at the same time as ensuring that he didn't come to any harm. Dad didn't know how to do both.

'I bet Mum wants me to.'

'She's dead, Brand. She doesn't want anything any more.'

He'd said it.

At last he'd said it, right out, to Brand.

Brand bit his lip, refusing to let himself cry. 'I'm going to practise some more,' he said defiantly.

'Wait!' Dad scrabbled up his drawings and hurried after Brand.

The cover with the revenant fell to the floor. Megan bent to pick it up. Behind her Alyson began singing softly. There were no real words to the song, only meaningless sounds. The tune, though, was clear enough. It was a simple sweet song and one that Megan had heard before.

'That's where I heard *The Ivy Crown* first!' Stripped of Paganini's embellishments and the morris men's jinglings, Megan's unmusical ear recognised the tune at last. 'You sang it the day I met you.'

'Yes, I did. I'd seen Jacob in your room and thought you might be receptive to his presence. I simply tried to move things along a bit, plant a musical hint.

'At first I thought Brand, being the musician, might be of use to me, then I heard about about his reluctance to play the violin any more and I decided he couldn't help me. You had to do instead. I made the mistake of assuming that you're as musical as your brother. I didn't realise you had a tin ear.'

Diminished, Megan stayed silent.

'Brand will have to do after all,' the housekeeper added, 'even though he's a boy.'

'You used me,' Megan accused. 'You used me to help Brand find the violin. You never cared about me at all.'

'I did care, and for a very good reason. Now, let's get out of The House and go for a walk to get some air. We'll talk this through.'

Megan did want to get away and think. What she didn't want was Alyson's company. If only she were strong enough to say so.

Alyson led Megan across the expanse of bracken. The wishing tree blazed with afternoon sunlight, its scarlet tokens burning like innumerable small flames. Megan looked to one side as they passed the looming bulk of the bonfire. Alyson settled on one of the tree's gnarled old roots. Clusters of red-spotted toadstools sprouted round her feet like exotic flowers.

Megan sat a little way off on a cushion of newly fallen leaves. All around her others drifted quiet as snowflakes to the ground. One caught in Alyson's hair, burning like a golden flame against the silky black.

'Poor Megan.'

Megan didn't want Alyson's sympathy.

'Left to cope alone after your mother died,' Alyson said, 'with all your father's attention on Brand. It wasn't right.'

Although Alyson spoke the truth it was only part of the truth. Megan didn't know how to express that so she stayed mute.

'You needn't feel guilty because you're treated badly.'

Alyson had gone too far. Dad tried not to dump responsibility on her. It happened that way because she made him think she was fine, able to cope without him. She did it on purpose because she had something to hide that even Alyson wasn't going to get her to confess to.

All the same: 'Dad never says sorry about not having time for me any more. He never really listens to me, not like Mum did.'

'I've got time. I'll listen.' Alyson spoke gently, sincerely.

136

Megan already regretted complaining about Dad. A sensation of disloyalty slithered round her heart. 'I haven't got anything to say,' she mumbled.

'Nothing? No fears, no regrets, no wishes even?'

'Making wishes is stupid,' Megan said quickly.

'Is it? Perhaps you're right.' The golden eyes were sympathetic. 'But if you could, what would you wish for most in all the world?'

The invitation was irresistible. 'I'd like to be able to say goodbye properly to my mother.'

'You have unfinished business.'

You could say that: business that was going to haunt Megan for ever because she'd never be able to tell Mum how sorry she was for making her a promise she had no intention of keeping.

'I can help you,' Alyson said. 'I can make it possible for you to see your mother and speak to her.'

'You're crazy!'

'I can do it — if you do something for me in return. I want to put right what was done to Judith and I need Brand.'

'No.' Megan knew what Alyson wanted. 'He's not going to play *The Ivy Crown* tomorrow. Dad won't let him.'

'He won't come to any harm.'

'I heard Mr Walmsley say Jacob was dangerous. He'll hurt Brand.'

'He won't be able to. He's too frightened of me. If you persuade your father to let Brand play, I'll make sure you see your mother again.'

It was a horrible suggestion, to allow Alyson to use her little brother in exchange for seeing her dead mother.

'No!'

A rogue wind rippled round the dancing ring. The tree flexed its branches and its leaves fell faster.

Megan tensed, ready to fly if the tree started to shudder again or cry out. Nothing happened, except that in those few quiet seconds while she listened to the calming purl of the leaves above her, Megan thought of Judith — killed for an offence she didn't commit; her soul imprisoned on earth; powerless to help herself. It had been such a long, long time. Someone had to set Judith free.

'All right, I'll do it.'

Alyson bestowed her most enchanting smile on Megan. 'And I'll grant your wish.'

'No you won't. It's right to try and help Judith if we can, Brand and me, but we don't need anything from you.'

'If that's what you want.'

'Yes, it is.'

'Very well.' Alyson brushed leaves from her skirt. 'I think your father might need quite a bit of persuading. The sooner you go and do it the better.'

Alyson's command came wrapped up in butter-smooth cadences. It was much more dishonest than Brian Walmsley's way of speaking. He always meant exactly what he said even if the way he said it made you want to grind your teeth.

'It's important,' Alyson pressed. 'There isn't much time and I really care about what happens to Judith. At times I feel almost as if she really is my sister.'

Megan didn't believe her, not now she understood exactly how Alyson manipulated people to get what she wanted.

'What did you mean earlier when you said you cared about me for a good reason?' Megan asked.

Alyson stepped up her attempts at sincerity, her eyes looking unwaveringly into Megan's: 'I don't have a daughter of my own to pass Judith's story on to. You coming here meant I could ask for your help. I was sure you'd say yes once you understood.'

That was Alyson's idea of caring? Using Megan as a substitute daughter so she could cast a spell. Megan felt a rush of fury at herself for allowing Alyson's trickery to fool her. Perhaps it was her turn to fool Alyson?

'I'll go and talk to Dad now.'

'Good. As I said, we don't have much time. Brand has to play tomorrow night.'

'For Judith's sake.'

'That's right,' Alyson said as though she were congratulating Megan on learning a complicated set of instructions perfectly.

Megan got up from the cushion of leaves. 'I want to be on my own for a bit.'

She strode across the dancing ring away from Alyson, away from the menacing stack of the fire, away from the woods.

She reached The House and lifted the latch on the door. The raven's cry sawed at the air behind her.

In the hall Pywackett waited. She snarled at Megan.

Outside or inside there was no getting away from Alyson.

Megan lay unsleeping in her box. She played the argument she'd had with Dad over and over in her head.

'Dabbling with the supernatural is dangerous,' he'd said. 'Brian's always known that. He wanted Alyson to drop this obsession with revenge and she wouldn't. Now she's trying to make you and Brand go along with her mad idea.'

'We've still got to help Judith,' Megan said. 'What Jacob did was wrong. We can't let him get away with it And we can't let Judith go on suffering for ever.'

Dad didn't have an answer to that. He gave in. As though unable to stand up to Megan-the-angel defying him he said, 'All right, Brand can play the violin tomorrow.'

Abruptly he walked away, his gait curiously deflated and unsure. It had hurt Megan to see it

A shadow blocked the faint light stroking the fabric walls.

'Megan.'

She twitched the curtains apart. Brand climbed aboard and she rose a little on the unexpected tide. She pulled the curtains to, enclosing them safely in the snug four-poster den. Brand leaned against her wrapped in the leaf-patterned duvet he'd dragged in with him. His eyes glinted in his shadowed face.

'I'm scared about tomorrow night.'

'I am too,' Megan said. 'I think we all are. The same as Paganini was. Remember when Jacob threatened him? He was so scared he left The House the next day.'

'Paganini didn't know about Judith. I bet he'd have tried to help if he had.' He buried his face against Megan's shoulder. 'I'm only a bit scared.' His voice came out muffled.

Megan bit at her lip. Perhaps she was being a user now, like Alyson: encouraging Brand to play to help her set Judith free. She made herself say, 'Maybe you ought to think again.'

'No!' Brand's head lifted. 'I've got to play, for Judith. Don't you understand?'

Megan shook her head.

'I didn't play for Mum, I didn't practise like she wanted, and she died.'

Megan couldn't bear the stricken look on Brand's face.

'She didn't die because you behaved like a normal boy and wouldn't practise your violin! How can you think that? Nothing could've saved Mum, nothing. Everybody tried, the doctors, everybody. You couldn't make any difference, not even Dad could make any difference.'

He wasn't convinced. 'I didn't play for Mum but I am going to play for Judith. Mum wants me to, I know it.'

Fear made a grab for Megan's heart 'I'll look after you,' she promised, 'and so will Dad.'

'Can I stay here tonight?'

'Course you can.' Megan tucked the duvet round him.

'You're safe with me.'

She watched until he fell asleep. It didn't take long. He was worn out. But sleep didn't come to her that easily. Memories of Mum kept her awake. The more she tried to chase them away the more they jostled and clamoured for attention. They were all of Mum's last night, though no one had known it at the time: the doctors had said it would be days.

It had been Megan's turn to sit with her. At first Mum was asleep, then her eyes opened quite suddenly. 'Brand, bring Brand to play for me.'

'All right.'

With a struggle Mum smiled gratefully. It terrified Megan, that spasm passing over Mum's face, masquerading as a smile. And Mum saw the fear in her face because Megan hadn't learned then how to smother a feeling at the instant it began.

Mum stopped trying to smile. 'Promise me,' she breathed.

'I promise,' Megan the deceiver said, and fled.

She stayed in her room: ten minutes, half an hour, an hour, all the time saying, 'I'll go in a minute. Just a bit longer, then I'll fetch Brand.'

She hadn't been able to. She told herself he'd be too afraid, she knew he would. So she stayed in her room while downstairs Dad worked at his latest project and Brand listened to Gran read a story.

And that was when Mum died, all alone because of Megan.

She curled up against Brand's warm little body.

She'd had no right to decide what was best for him. If only she'd kept her promise he'd never have got this stupid, terrible idea that he'd somehow stopped Mum from getting better. And there was nothing she could do about it, nothing, it was too late.

But at least she'd made sure he was going to have his

chance to play for Judith tomorrow. That was something. And she'd see he wouldn't come to any harm.

Yes, she promised herself as she fell asleep at last, I can do that.

Jacob stayed away that night.

Duet

The owl winked at Megan. Although she knew it was only the effect of moonlight on bronze, she felt comforted. She stroked its head. 'I hope this works,' she whispered to the impassive little bird. She spoke softly so that no one in the group assembled in the hall could hear.

'It's time,' Alyson announced.

Brand began to play *The Ivy Crown*. Notes flowed through the hall, spiralling upwards to where the nine muses danced around the dome.

And suddenly, there in the middle of the hall, Jacob came dancing.

'We must go. Open the door,' ordered Alyson.

Dad swung the door wide.

Brand led the way across the hall and out through the door. Jacob followed, forced to obey the summons of the music. Alyson went next, then Megan and Dad.

Brand played the procession over the bridge, stumbling a little in the darkness. Megan ran in front of him. 'Follow me.'

Thanks.' His step steadied behind her and he quickened the tempo of his playing. Like a small Pied Piper he charmed his followers away from home. The gibbous moon and a sprinkling of stars were all that lit the way down familiar pathways as they marched obedient to his tune.

Megan led the line along sodden paths, past the river, over the grassy track. She smelled smoke, glimpsed a lick of orange and yellow. She reached the sweep of bracken. Next to the high black blot of the bonfire stood a man holding a flaming torch that snapped and smoked in the night air.

'Let's hope there's an end to this tonight,' Brian Walmsley said coldly to Alyson.

'Light the fire,' she said.

He turned and touched the torch to the waiting timber. For a moment small flames played hide-and-seek in the lattice of wood then, with a rush, they stretched out, surged upwards and roared away through the top. Fire filled the dancing ring with yellow light.

Jacob began to dance around the fire, slowly at first, capering a complicated pattern of half forgotten movements. He completed the first circle.

Alyson lifted her arms, 'Faster!'

Brand raised the tempo. Jacob danced by, a ridiculous old man footing a young man's steps. He completed the second circuit of the fire.

'Faster!' Alyson commanded. Reflected flame turned her eyes to molten gold.

Sweat stood out on Brand's forehead, trickled down his face. The rhythm increased. Jacob danced like a madman, arms and legs flailing. Round, round the execution fire he went on his final lap, ending at last where he'd begun.

Brand's music faded away. The scent of woodsmoke mingled with another, fouler smell. A terrible rending screamed in the air. The wishing tree swayed and trembled. Its bark split open, ripped back. From its gaping wound, glistening with sap, slid a woman. She stood up between the tree and the fire and shook out her scarlet skirts.

Judith Moone was Dad's picture to the life.

Alyson went to greet her. 'Welcome, sister.'

' Is Jacob Fisher here?' Judith's voice floated on the air, fragile as a moonbeam.

'He is.'

Alyson beckoned to a cowering Jacob: 'Say your piece, old man.'

Jacob crawled to the woman he had wronged three centuries before. His words when they came, creaked like an ancient oak. 'Forgive me.'

'For what, Jacob Fisher?'

'For saying you were a witch when you were a virtuous woman.'

'Why did you do it, Jacob?' Alyson demanded.

Never taking his eyes from Judith, the steward said, 'She spurned me. She made me appear a fool, a buffoon.'

'Still I forgive you,' Judith said. 'Go on your way.'

'I do not know it.'

Alyson pointed at the roaring flames. 'There lies your way.'

'No!'

Judith mirrored Alyson's gesture. 'You have far to go. Best be gone quickly.'

'No!'

Together the women walked towards Jacob. He backed away, closer, closer to the flames. Desperately he looked over his shoulder into the heart of the fire. He turned towards it, covered his eyes and ran into the flames.

In a second he was gone. Only the flames moved, like savouring tongues. Judith watched them intently.

Triumphantly Alyson said, 'You're free, Judith! Free to leave this place.'

'First, sister,' Judith said, 'there is something I must do. For centuries I've listened to the wishes of all those who tied their tokens of desire on to my branches. There have been so many that I learned to see into a heart before it even opened to me. I know what's in yours and it's dangerous. You yearn for the power of magic and you must not have it. I have to take it from you, to the other side of the fire.'

'You can't! You mustn't!' Alyson backed away, horror turning her eyes feral.

'I must and I will.'

With a snarl of despair Alyson fled away into the midnight trees.

Impassively Judith said, 'It's done.'

She gestured with a sweep of her arms. The fire sprang into sheets of golden flame: they parted.

'Listen carefully, little daughter,' she said to Megan, 'there will be a message for you. For all of you.' Then Judith turned her back on the world at last and walked gladly through the flames to the place beyond.

Through the open curtains of fire came music of such beauty that Megan felt it was almost more than she could bear. Beside her, Brand lifted his violin. He played a questioning note.

In reply, a lament — regretful, sorrowing — filled the glade.

In the music Megan heard her mother speak her name.

I'm sorry, Megan's guilty heart cried out, I'm sorry I didn't do what I promised.

The music comforted her, told her it understood.

I couldn't bring Brand to you, Megan said. He was too afraid. And so was I. I couldn't do it. I couldn't keep my promise.

But you have, the music said. Here he is, playing for me, playing as I always knew he could.

The music from both sides of the fire wove together, rose in harmony above the flames, streamed away into the night and mingled with the stars.

Slowly the swags of flame drew together. The music from the world beyond the fire faded softly and Brand's accompanying diminuendo died away in perfect unison. The two halves of the fire met, flared briefly, then dropped back.

The forest stood silent except for the snapping of flames and the crackling of burning wood.

Megan turned to her family. 'Mum's forgiven me.'

'And me,' Brand said.

'And me,' said Dad. 'I think it's time to go home.'

Megan stroked the wishing tree's ancient bark. There was no sign of the fissure that had split it open the night before.

She walked round the tree trailing her hand over its wide girth. She didn't know any longer which of the bright ribbons blossoming above her were the ones she'd tied. It didn't matter; her wishes had been granted. Robin would be pleased about that.

Megan leaned against the trunk, pressing her face to its woody skin. 'Thank you,' she said.

Now there was no presence in the tree to give an answering shiver.

'Megan!' Brian Walmsley walked over the battered bracken towards her. 'I see you're not scared of me any more.'

She ignored his fatuous grin. 'The ghosts have all gone.'

They walked in reasonably companionable silence for a while then Megan said, 'Mr Walmsley, what about the bonfire? I mean, the people in Stretton are going to wonder what happened to it.'

'No problem. They've been saying for some time it's too far to go just to build a fire. And they don't like what they call the "long" walk from the road to the dancing ring. Now that vandals have destroyed the bonfire before 5th November, they don't want any more to do with the woods. I'm helping to organise a proper firework display in the market square. Of course it's too short notice to be much good but next year it will be really great.'

'Who said vandals set light to the fire last night?'

The flexible smile stretched back over Brian Walmsley's very white teeth making him look something like a shark. 'No idea.'

As if, Megan thought.

They'd reached The House. 'Your father told me you're

147

going home in a day or two,' Brian Walmsley said.

'Brand and I want to get back to school, especially me. And Dad's working like mad on his novel. He said it's not often you get a whole story given to you on a plate complete with pictures.'

'I can see there's no point in staying if you don't have to. I'll miss you all though.'

Could he mean what he said?

'It's not often I get a winter booking,' he went on. 'Yours was a real bonus. And of course, you did find the Guarneri which makes up for anything, including terminating your lease early. By the way, Daniel Turner said Brand can keep that violin he borrowed for as long as he wants to. He told me to tell him, Keep practising.'

'He will.'

Brian Walmsley headed for his car.

'Aren't you coming in?' Megan asked in surprise.

'I've got to go and set up the advertising for a new housekeeper. Alyson resigned this morning.'

'What's she going to do?'

'No idea.'

Brian Walmsley got into his car and wound down the window. 'I probably won't have time to come and say goodbye. I'll ring your father but give him and Brand my best wishes anyway. And good luck to you, Megan.'

He drove off in a flourish of gravel.

Megan watched the car until it went over the hill. It felt strange to think she wouldn't see him again. Not that she'd miss him.

Oh well, whatever, she'd seen the last of Brian Walmsley.

But she hadn't.

Last Movement

The powerful sweet sound of the Guarneri Del Gesù violin reached into every corner of the ballroom. As the last notes of Paganini's *Variation on the Theme of the Ivy Crown* faded away the audience broke into applause.

Brand bowed under the mocking gaze of Paganini whose portrait hung above him on the wall.

People began to move towards the dais which Brian Walmsley had had built as part of the ballroom's restoration. Dad quickly used his bulk and height to bully his way through the push of media representatives to his son's side.

What's he worrying for? Megan thought, Brand's enjoying every minute. And anyway, there's the goons. She couldn't help smiling as the two enormous bodyguards Brian Walmsley had hired to mind the Guarneri moved closer to Brand.

Megan wove her way out of the ballroom over the snaking mass of TV cables and into the hall of The House in The Hollow. She stood on the bottom step of the stairs and stroked the owl's unruffled feathers. Hot summer sun struck his open eye with the force of a gong beat. The eye beamed upwards to the dome where Megan could see Euterpe playing her lyre. The TV crew had struggled a bit getting their equipment up there to film Megan pointing out the muse and reciting Lettice's poem.

'They probably won't even use what they filmed,' Megan told the owl.

She wasn't sure whether that pleased her or not. Did she really want to be a celebrity, even for five minutes?

She sat on the bottom step and leaned against the newel

149

post. On the whole, she decided, Brand coped better with all this attention than she did. Although they never discussed what Mum had said to them in the forest, Brand did tell Megan one thing: during his duet with Mum he'd discovered what music was really about. He wanted to play seriously now and practised whenever he could. Playing in public was a big treat.

Brian Walmsley came out of the ballroom. He sat down next to Megan, propping himself up against the owl-less post He pulled out his crisp handkerchief and wiped his face. What an idiot, wearing a suit in the middle of summer.

'Shouldn't you be in there, organising?' she asked.

'It's all under control. Your father's got Brand's interviews lined up for later. You've already done yours. Daniel's done his on restoring the violin and I've done mine on The Sanctuary Trust's plans for its future use. With a bit of luck everybody will be packed up and gone by this evening. It's been a pretty good few days.'

Brian Walmsley had done a brilliant publicity job for The Trust but, watching his self-satisfied expression, Megan knew she'd never admit it to him. There was one thing she had to say though.

'Thanks for letting Brand play *The Ivy Crown* today. I know The Trust wanted somebody really famous to do it.'

Brian Walmsley gave her a half-strength grin. 'He did all Daniel asked and practised hard so I thought we'd let him, just this once. But I really let Brand do it because it was what you wanted. The Guarneri might never have seen the light of day again if it hadn't been for you and the only thing you asked for in return was a chance for your brother to play it.'

He wiped his face again. The mopping action seemed to pull the corners of his mouth outwards so Megan got the smile on full power as he said, 'I'm organising a competition for promising young virtuosi. The winner will get the

Guarneri for three years to help consolidate their careers.'

'I thought The Trust might sell the violin,' Megan said. 'I bet you'd have got enough to restore the whole House.'

Brian Walmsley flapped her comment away. 'We made sufficient from the sale of the Paganini manuscript to restore the ballroom, which was the most pressing job. And the violin loan scheme's first-class publicity: a competition every three years will give The Trust a permanently high profile. Donations have increased significantly since the story broke.'

A morose camera crew trooped out of the ballroom, trampling back over the lane of muck it had laid down when it came in.

'Oi! You lot!' A woman in jeans and a T-shirt flew out after them. 'Watch these tiles, they're Victorian originals, not do-it-yourself.'

'You know, that housekeeper's really very good,' Brian Walmsley said. 'I think I'll go and give her a hand supervising the exodus.'

Without even a goodbye to Megan, he followed the housekeeper back into the ballroom. As he went in, a familiar figure breezed out, braids swinging, beads clicking. 'What are you doing here?' Robin asked Megan.

Megan nodded towards the ballroom. 'Waiting for everybody to finish in there.'

'I've got to hang around for my dad, he's helping to clear up. Shall we go to the woods for a bit?'

'Good idea.' Megan patted the owl and followed Robin across the hall. She left The House behind her and went down to the river with Robin, to where sunlight pirouetted on the swirling water and birds sang in the summer trees.